MARVEL
SPIDEY
and his AMAZING FRIENDS

TEAM SPIDEY DOES IT ALL!

MARVEL

Los Angeles • New York

STORIES

MEET THE CHARACTERS

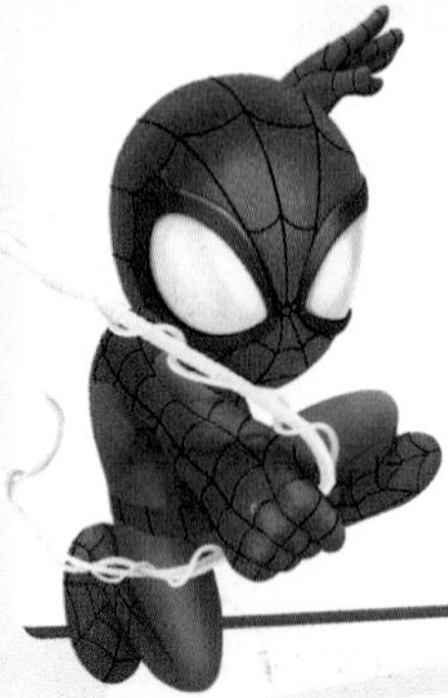

SPIDEY

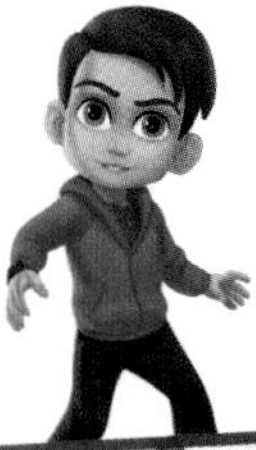

A SPECIAL SPIDER GAVE PETER PARKER SUPER POWERS. NOW HE FIGHTS VILLAINS AS SPIDEY!

MILES MORALES

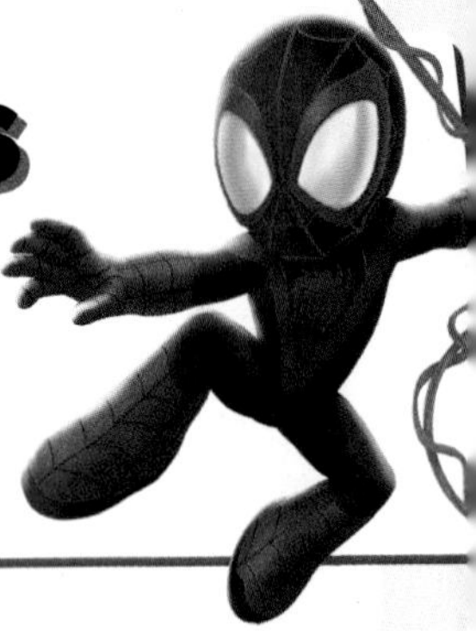

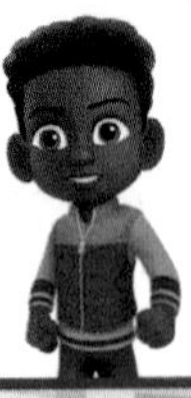

MILES MORALES IS ALWAYS READY TO LEAP INTO ACTION. HE CAN TURN INVISIBLE!

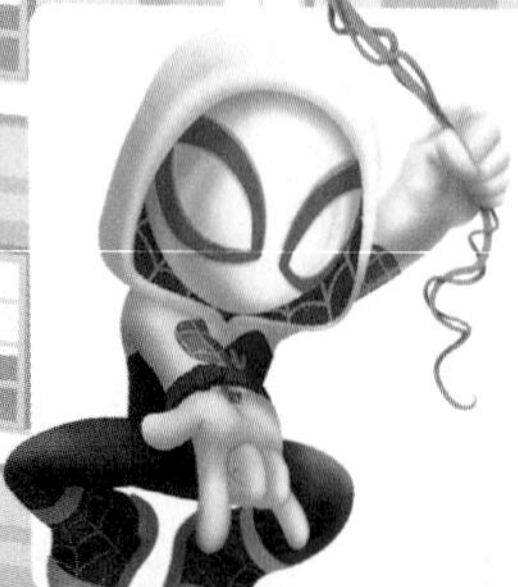

GHOST-SPIDER

GWEN STACY IS SUPER SMART. AS GHOST-SPIDER, SHE CAN GLIDE ON HER WEB WINGS.

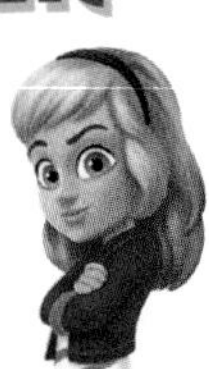

GREEN GOBLIN

GREEN GOBLIN PLAYS TRICKS! HE FLIES ON A GOBLIN GLIDER AND THROWS PUMPKIN PRANKS.

DOC OCK

DOC OCK IS VERY SMART. SHE WANTS TO TAKE OVER THE CITY WITH HER METAL TENTACLES.

RHINO

RHINO IS BIG AND STRONG. HE LIKES TO RUN AND BREAK THINGS.

HOW TO READ A COMIC

Follow our easy guide, and you will be reading comics in no time!

a
b
c
d

SUDDENLY...
DON'T REMIND ME NOW JUST

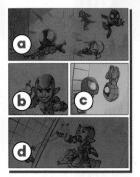

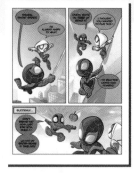

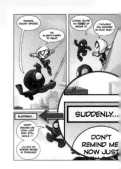

1 EACH PAGE OF A COMIC IS MADE UP OF PICTURES, OR PANELS. EACH PANEL TELLS ONE PART OF THE STORY.

2 THE CHARACTERS SPEAK IN WORD BALLOONS. THE POINTER OR TAIL AT THE END OF THE BALLOON SHOWS WHO IS SPEAKING.

3 SOMETIMES YO WILL SEE WORD IN A BOX. THAT I CALLED A CAPTION. CAPTIONS HELP TELL THE STORY AND TELL YOU THINGS YOU NE TO KNOW, LIKE TIME OR LOCATION.

THANKS, GHOST SPIDER!
I'M ALWAYS HAPPY TO HELP!
C'MON, GUYS! I'M TIRED OF BEING IT!
I THOUGHT YOU WANTED TO PLAY TAG--
--TO PRACTICE USING OUR POWERS!
DON'T REMIND ME! NOW JUST STAY STILL WHILE I--
UH-OH! MY SPIDER-SENSE IS TINGLING!

A PUMPKIN BOMB! GREEN GOBLIN MUST BE HERE!
CAN I JOIN YOUR GAME, WEB-HEADS?
BAM
NOT IF YOU TRY AND BLOW US UP!
NOW, WOULD I DO THAT?
YES!
LET'S PLAY SOMETHING ELSE, GOBLIN!
I DON'T LIKE THIS GAME!

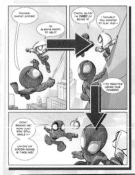

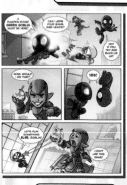

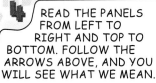

4 READ THE PANELS FROM LEFT TO RIGHT AND TOP TO BOTTOM. FOLLOW THE ARROWS ABOVE, AND YOU WILL SEE WHAT WE MEAN.

5 NOW SWING ON AND READ!

MEET THE HEROES!

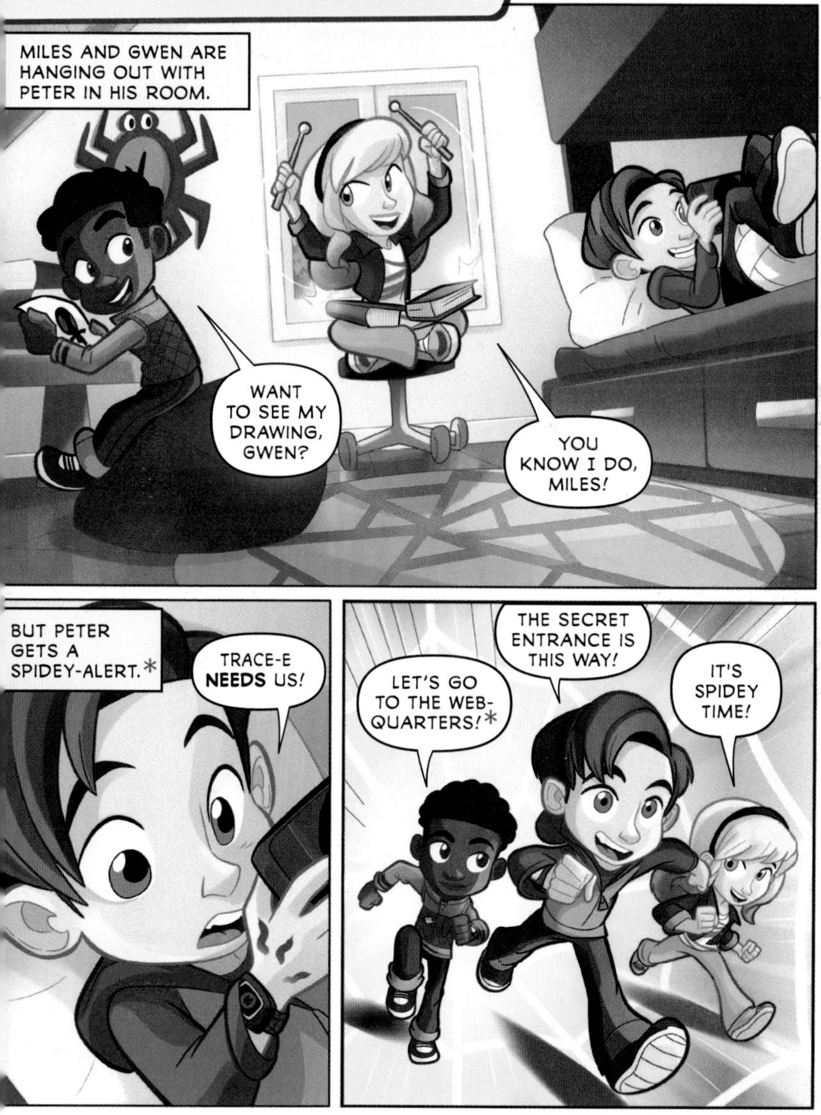

MILES AND GWEN ARE HANGING OUT WITH PETER IN HIS ROOM.
WANT TO SEE MY DRAWING, GWEN?
YOU KNOW I DO, MILES!
BUT PETER GETS A SPIDEY-ALERT.*
TRACE-E **NEEDS** US!
THE SECRET ENTRANCE IS THIS WAY!
LET'S GO TO THE WEB-QUARTERS!*
IT'S SPIDEY TIME!

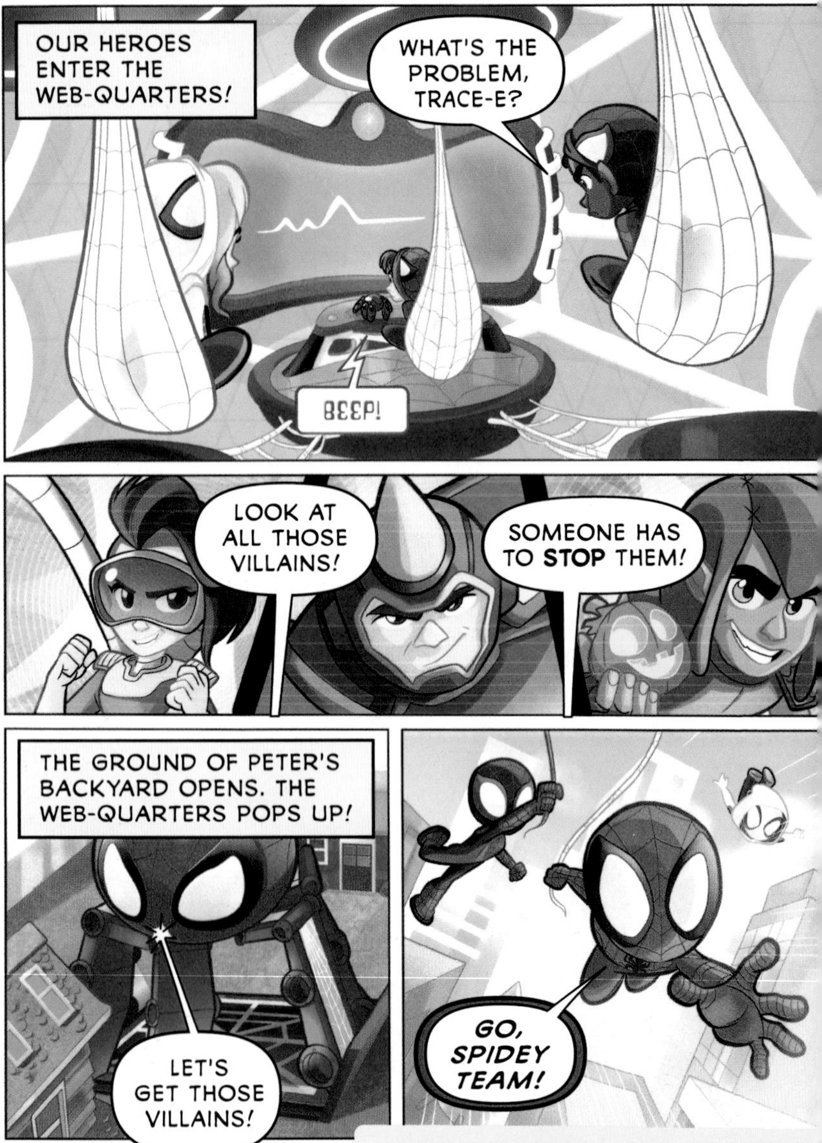

OUR HEROES ENTER THE WEB-QUARTERS!
WHAT'S THE PROBLEM, TRACE-E?
BEEP!
LOOK AT ALL THOSE VILLAINS!
SOMEONE HAS TO **STOP** THEM!
THE GROUND OF PETER'S BACKYARD OPENS. THE WEB-QUARTERS POPS UP!
LET'S GET THOSE VILLAINS!
GO, SPIDEY TEAM!
THE ADVENTURE BEGINS!

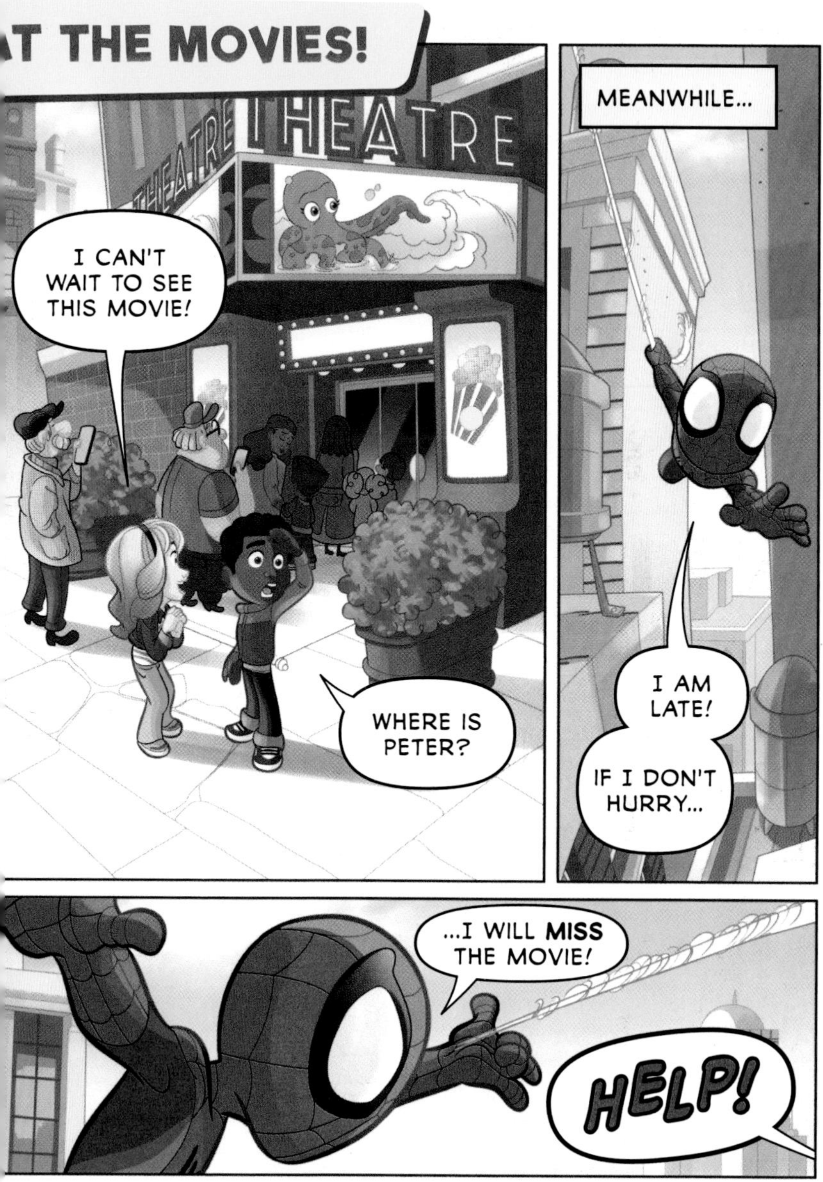

AT THE MOVIES!
THEATRE
THEATRE
I CAN'T WAIT TO SEE THIS MOVIE!
WHERE IS PETER?
MEANWHILE...
I AM LATE!
IF I DON'T HURRY...
...I WILL **MISS** THE MOVIE!
HELP!

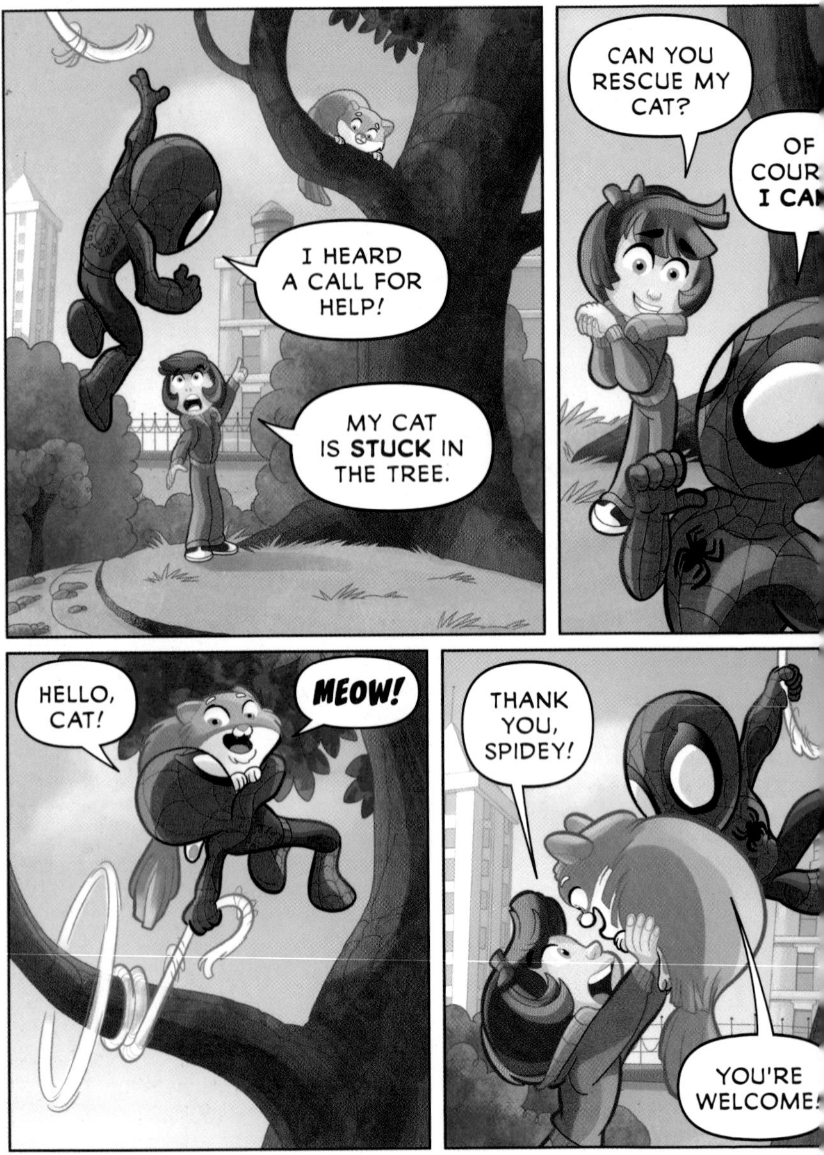
I HEARD A CALL FOR HELP!
MY CAT IS **STUCK** IN THE TREE.
CAN YOU RESCUE MY CAT?
OF COUR **I CA**
HELLO, CAT!
MEOW!
THANK YOU, SPIDEY!
YOU'RE WELCOME!

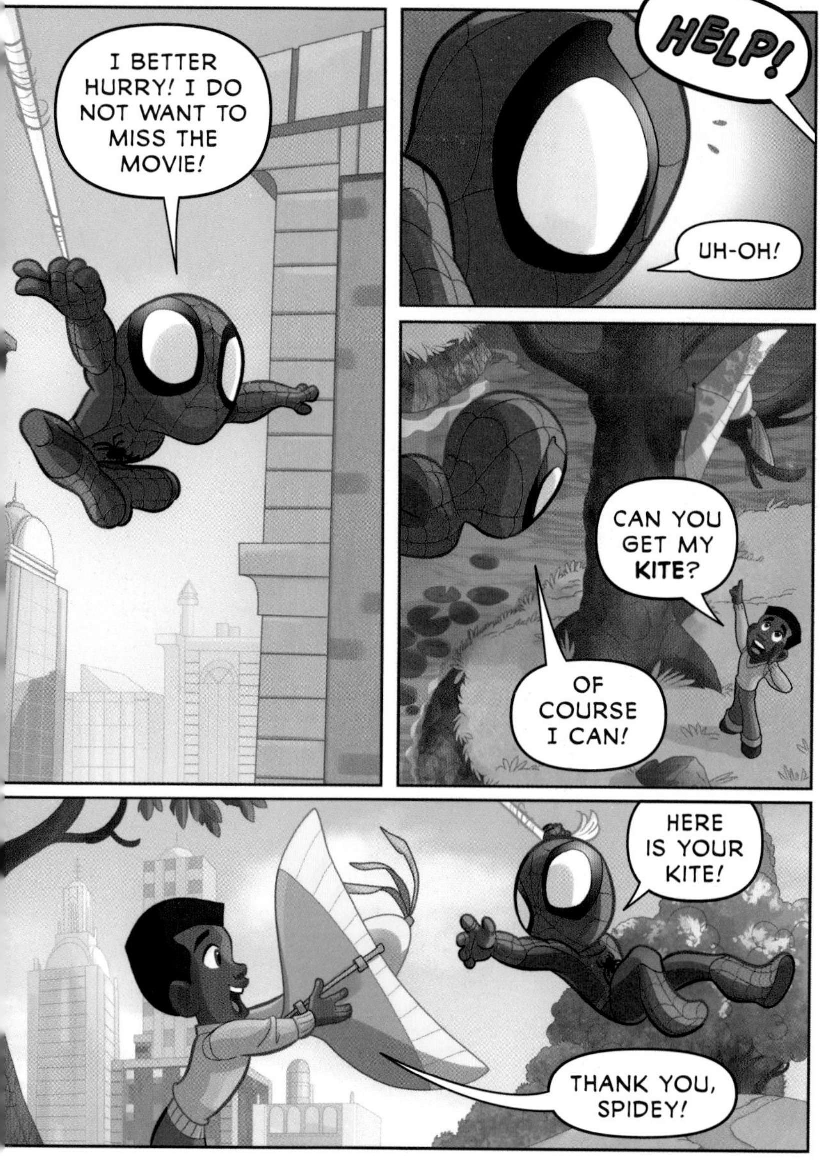
I BETTER HURRY! I DO NOT WANT TO MISS THE MOVIE!
HELP!
UH-OH!
CAN YOU GET MY **KITE**?
OF COURSE I CAN!
HERE IS YOUR KITE!
THANK YOU, SPIDEY!

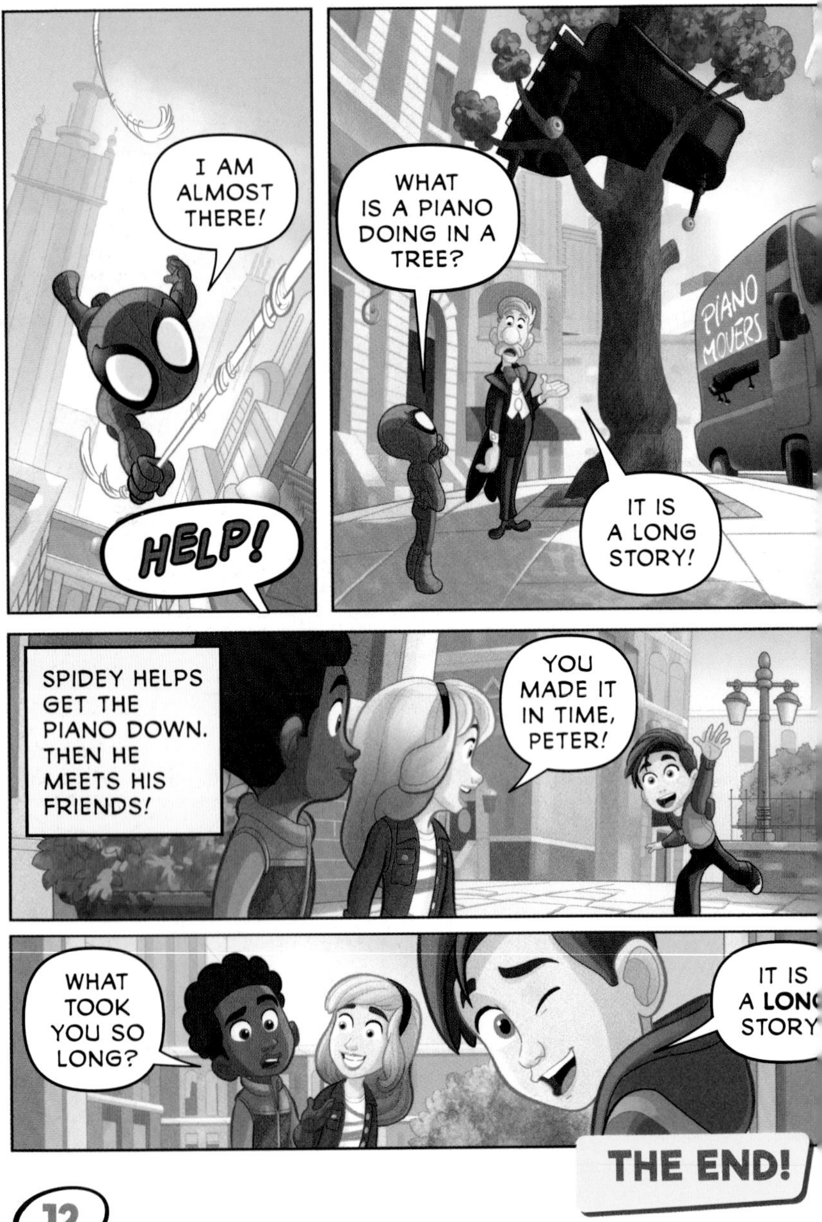
I AM ALMOST THERE!
HELP!
WHAT IS A PIANO DOING IN A TREE?
PIANO MOVERS
IT IS A LONG STORY!
SPIDEY HELPS GET THE PIANO DOWN. THEN HE MEETS HIS FRIENDS!
YOU MADE IT IN TIME, PETER!
WHAT TOOK YOU SO LONG?
IT IS A **LONG** STORY!
THE END!

WHERE'S MILES?

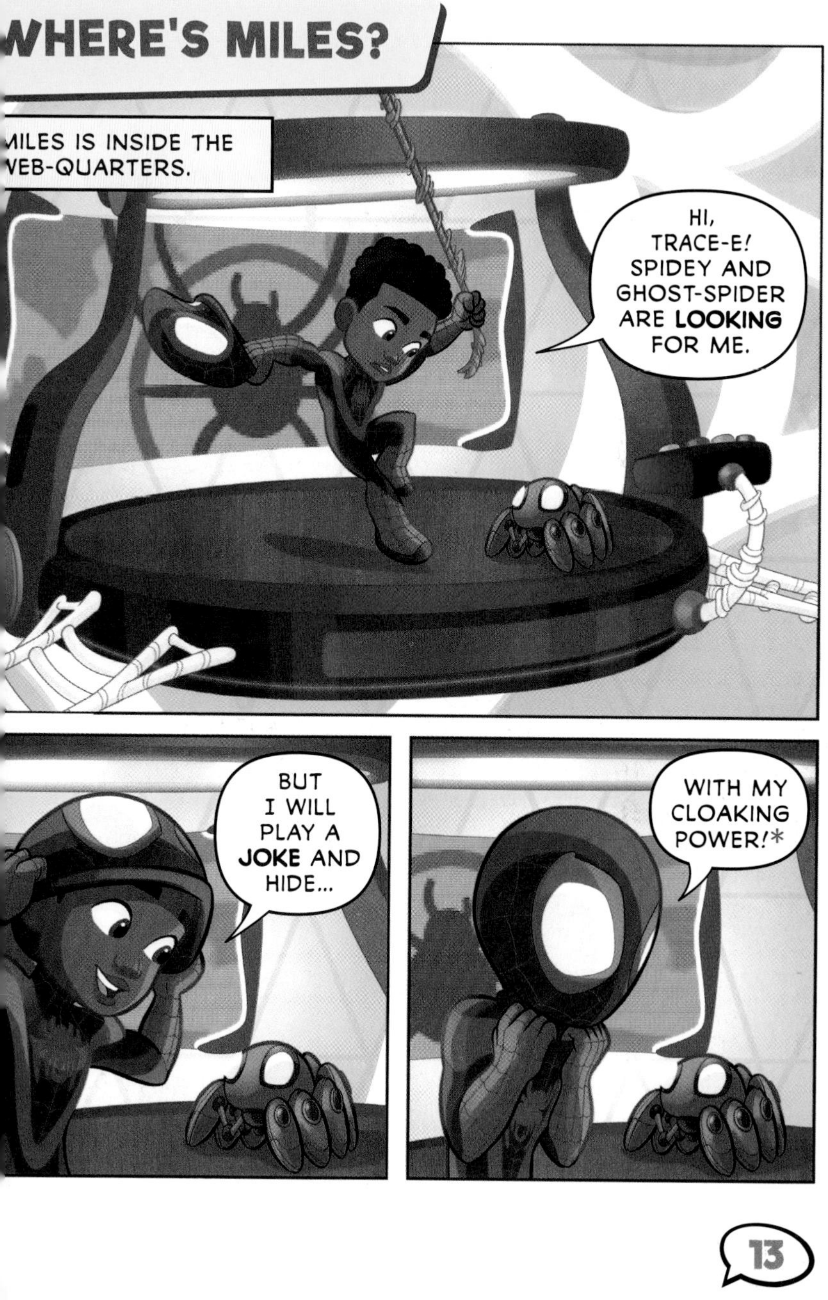

MILES IS INSIDE THE WEB-QUARTERS.
HI, TRACE-E! SPIDEY AND GHOST-SPIDER ARE **LOOKING** FOR ME.
BUT I WILL PLAY A **JOKE** AND HIDE...
WITH MY CLOAKING POWER!*

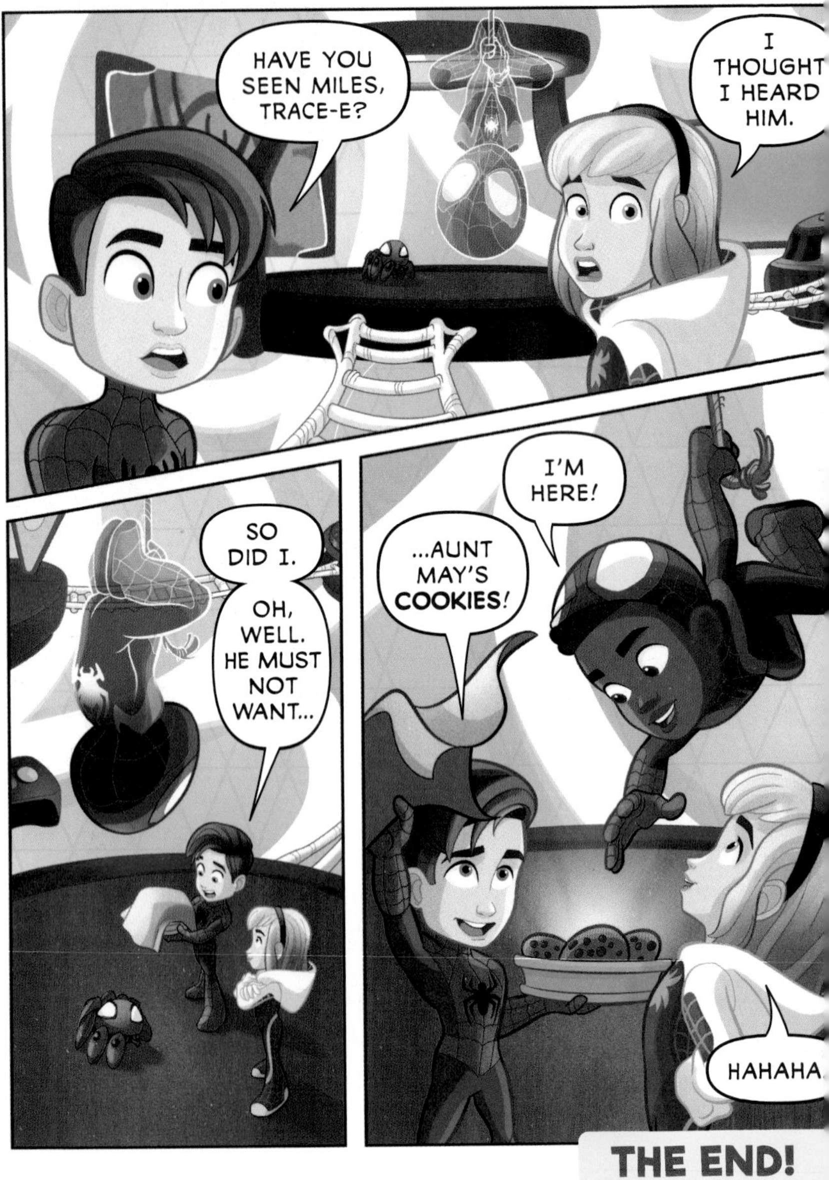

HAVE YOU SEEN MILES, TRACE-E?
I THOUGHT I HEARD HIM.
SO DID I.
OH, WELL. HE MUST NOT WANT...
I'M HERE!
...AUNT MAY'S COOKIES!
HAHAHA
THE END!

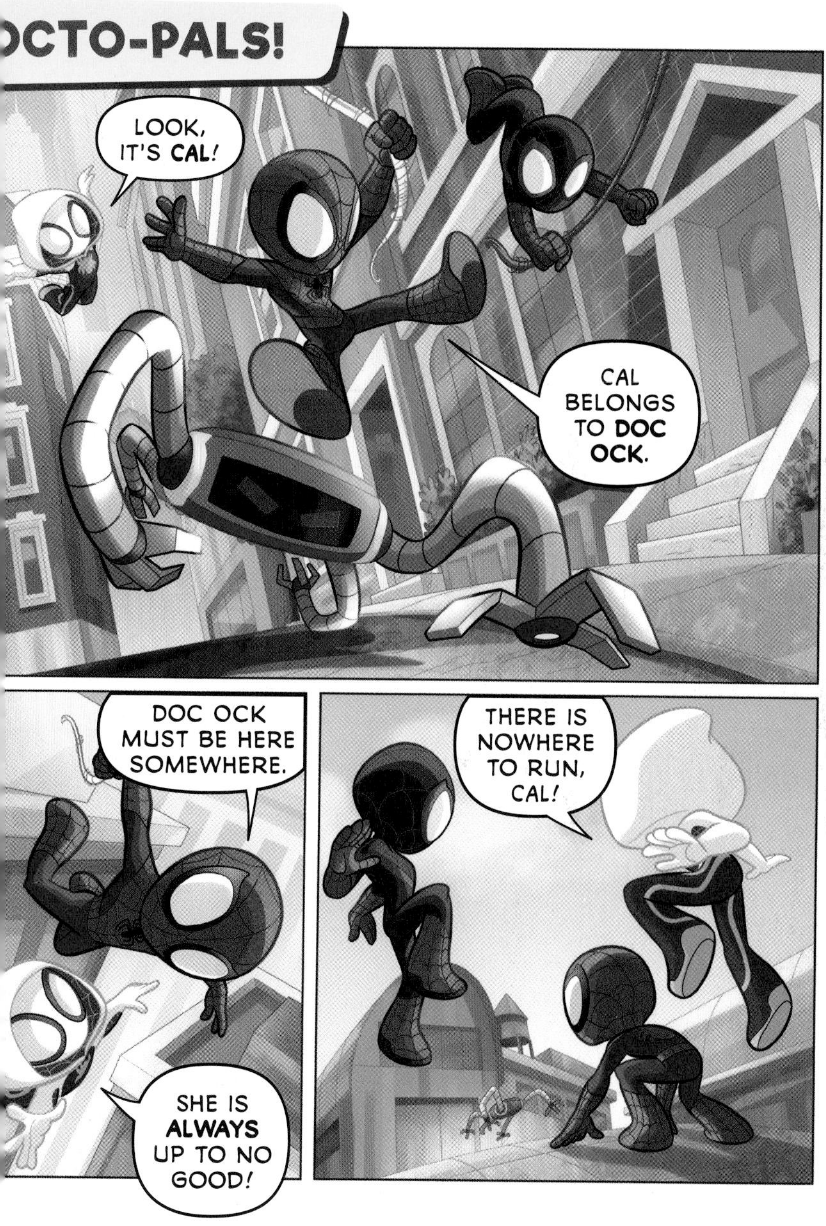
OCTO-PALS!
LOOK, IT'S **CAL**!
CAL BELONGS TO **DOC OCK**.
DOC OCK MUST BE HERE SOMEWHERE.
SHE IS **ALWAYS** UP TO NO GOOD!
THERE IS NOWHERE TO RUN, CAL!

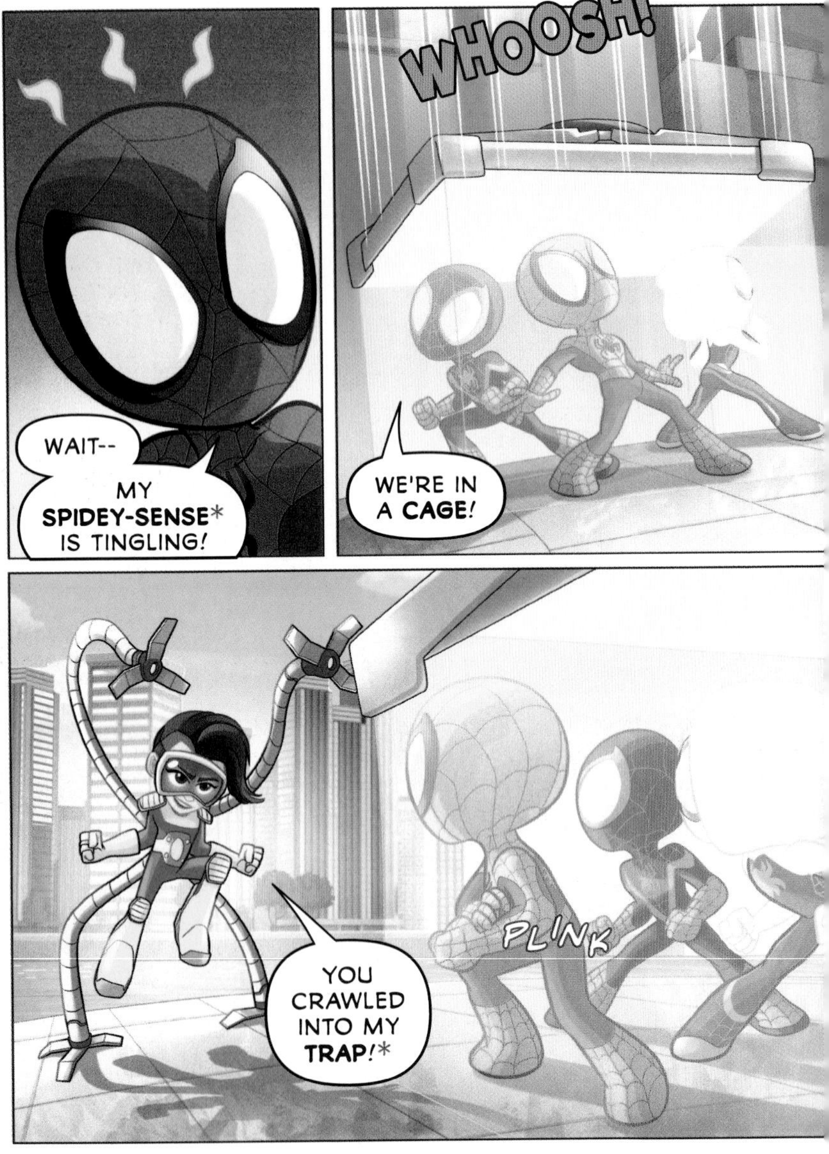
WAIT--
MY SPIDEY-SENSE* IS TINGLING!
WHOOSH!
WE'RE IN A CAGE!
YOU CRAWLED INTO MY TRAP!*
PLINK

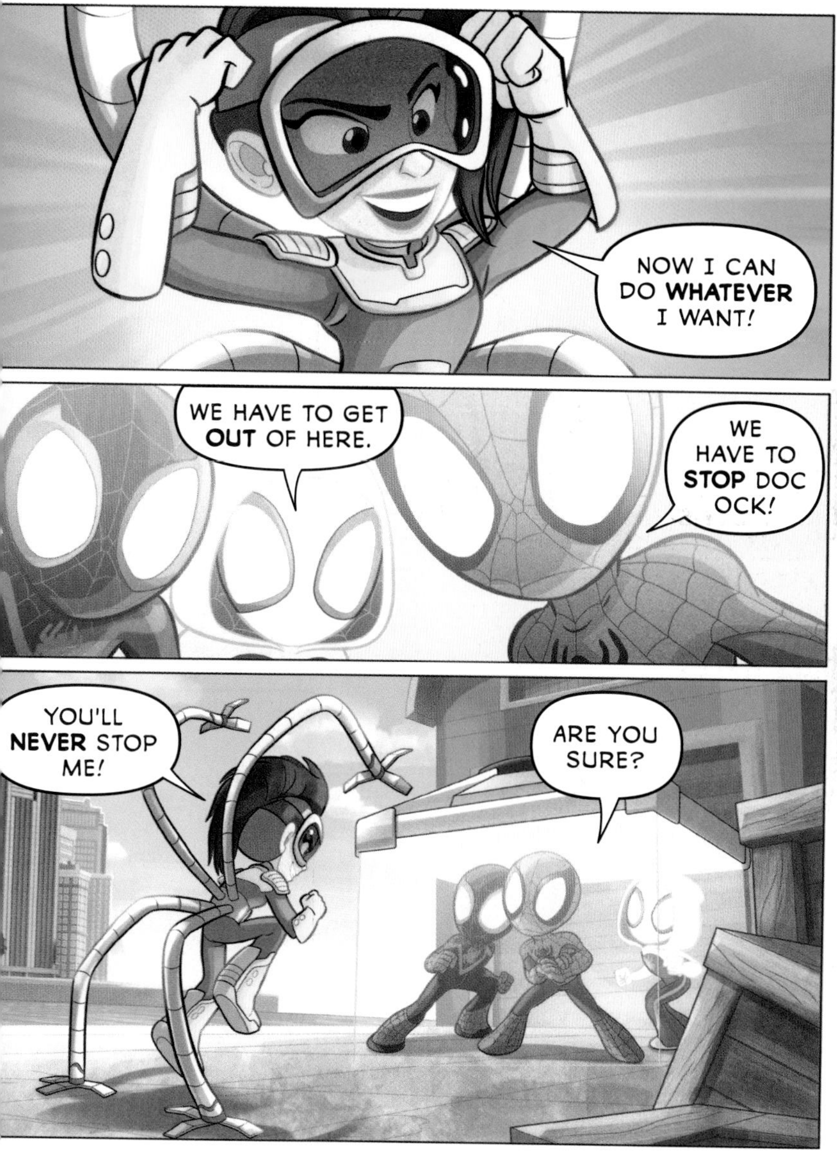
NOW I CAN DO **WHATEVER** I WANT!
WE HAVE TO GET **OUT** OF HERE.
WE HAVE TO **STOP** DOC OCK!
YOU'LL **NEVER** STOP ME!
ARE YOU SURE?

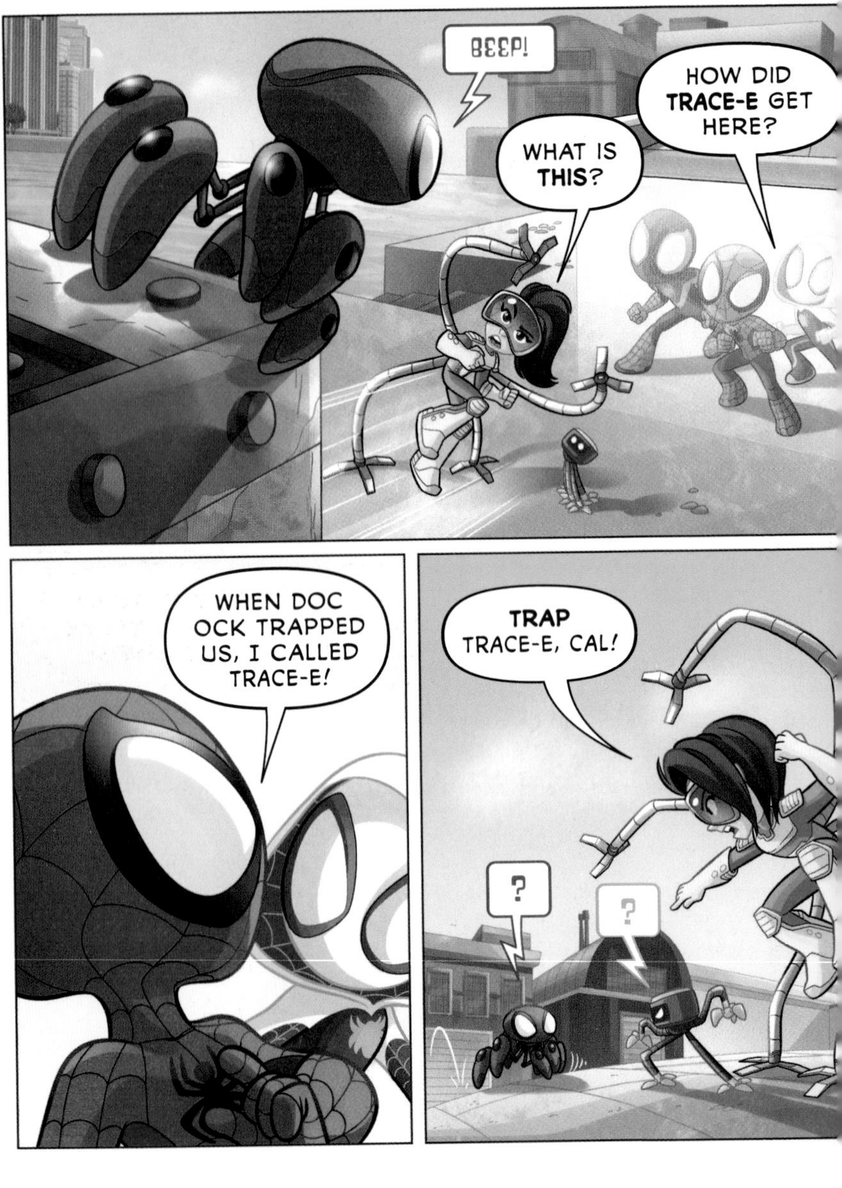
BEEP!
HOW DID TRACE-E GET HERE?
WHAT IS THIS?
WHEN DOC OCK TRAPPED US, I CALLED TRACE-E!
TRAP TRACE-E, CAL!
?
?

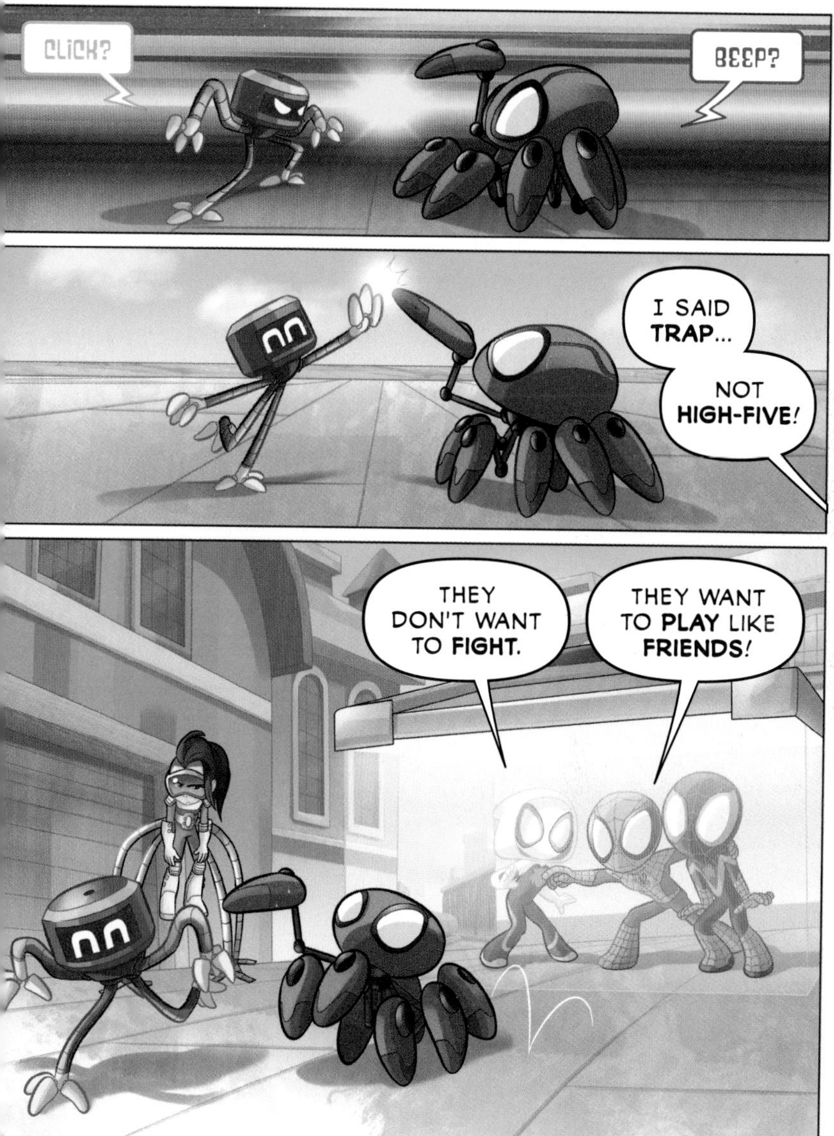
CLICK?
BEEP?
I SAID TRAP...
NOT HIGH-FIVE!
THEY DON'T WANT TO FIGHT.
THEY WANT TO PLAY LIKE FRIENDS!

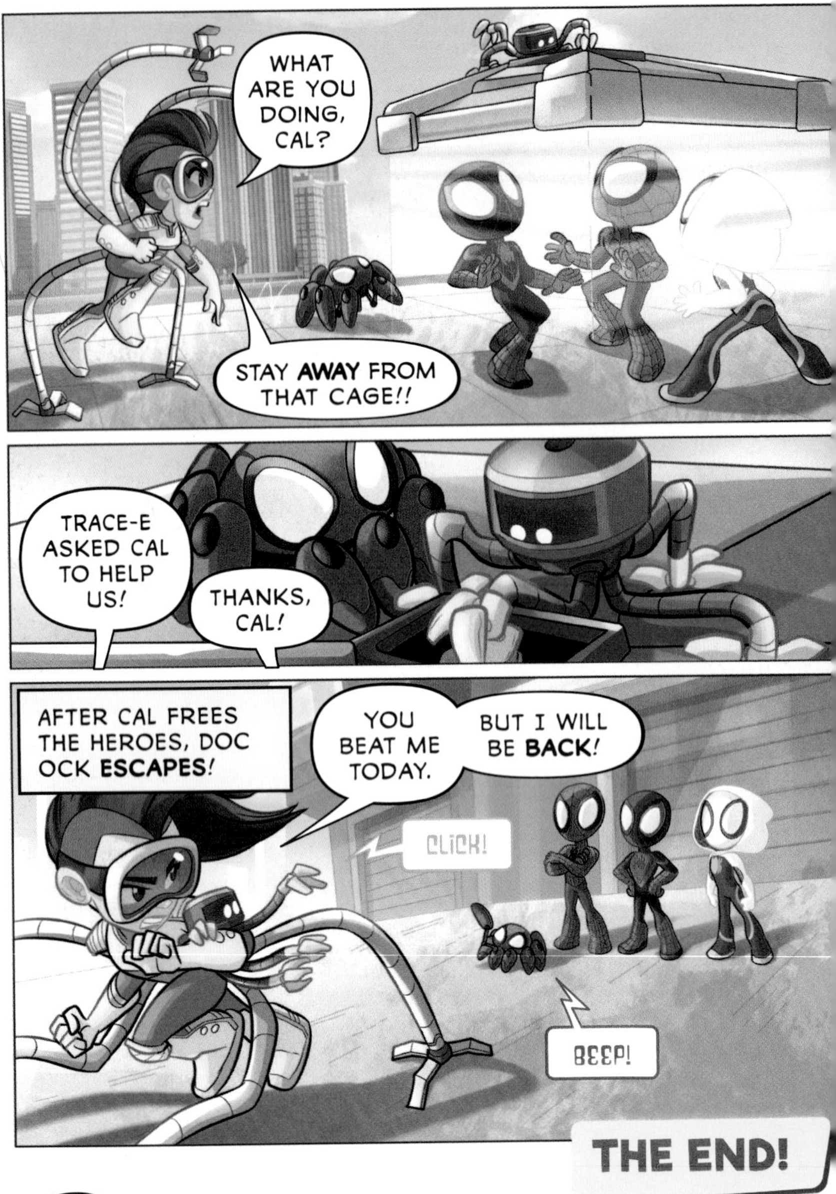
WHAT ARE YOU DOING, CAL?
STAY **AWAY** FROM THAT CAGE!!
TRACE-E ASKED CAL TO HELP US!
THANKS, CAL!
AFTER CAL FREES THE HEROES, DOC OCK **ESCAPES**!
YOU BEAT ME TODAY.
BUT I WILL BE **BACK**!
CLICK!
BEEP!
THE END!

TUMMY TROUBLE!

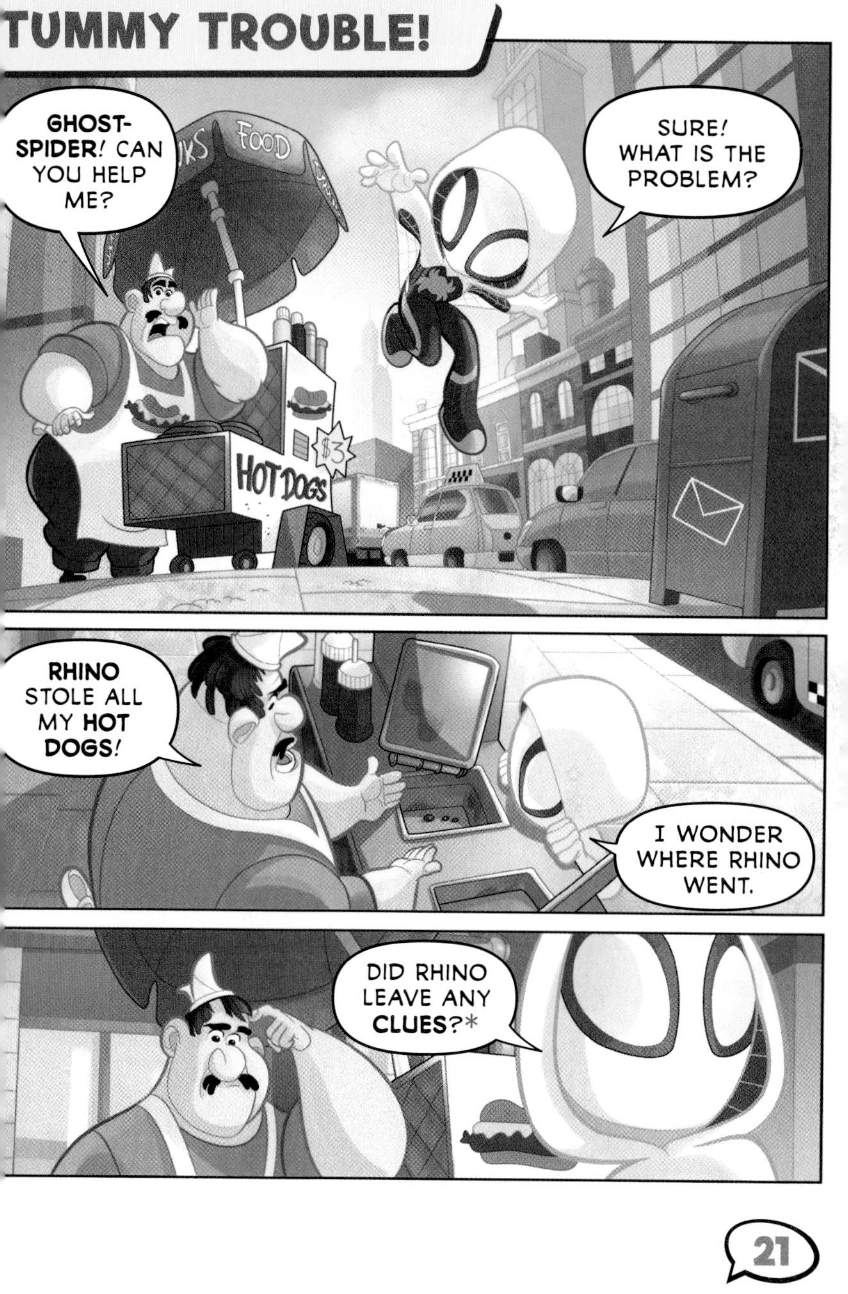
GHOST-SPIDER! CAN YOU HELP ME?
FOOD
HOT DOGS
$3
SURE! WHAT IS THE PROBLEM?
RHINO STOLE ALL MY HOT DOGS!
I WONDER WHERE RHINO WENT.
DID RHINO LEAVE ANY CLUES?*

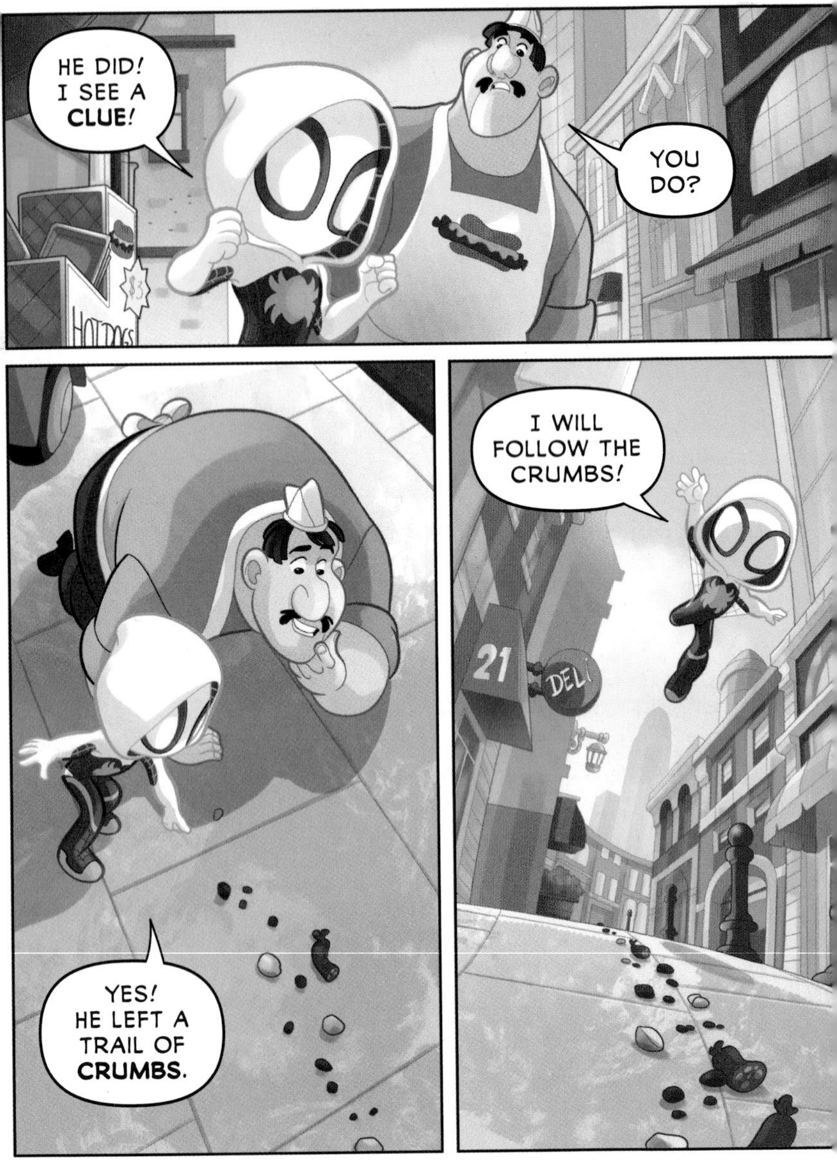
HE DID! I SEE A **CLUE**!
YOU DO?
HOT DOGS
$3
YES! HE LEFT A TRAIL OF **CRUMBS**.
I WILL FOLLOW THE CRUMBS!
21
DELI

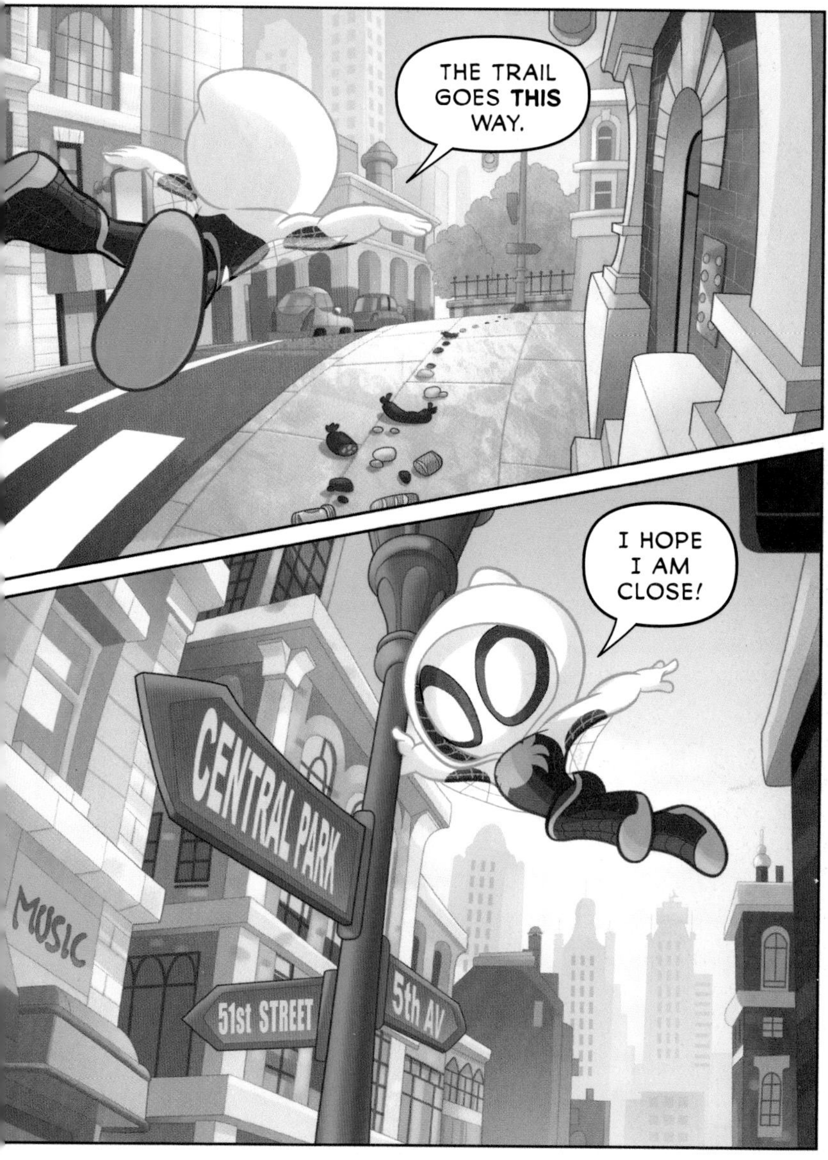
THE TRAIL GOES **THIS** WAY.
I HOPE I AM CLOSE!
CENTRAL PARK
MUSIC
51st STREET
5th AV

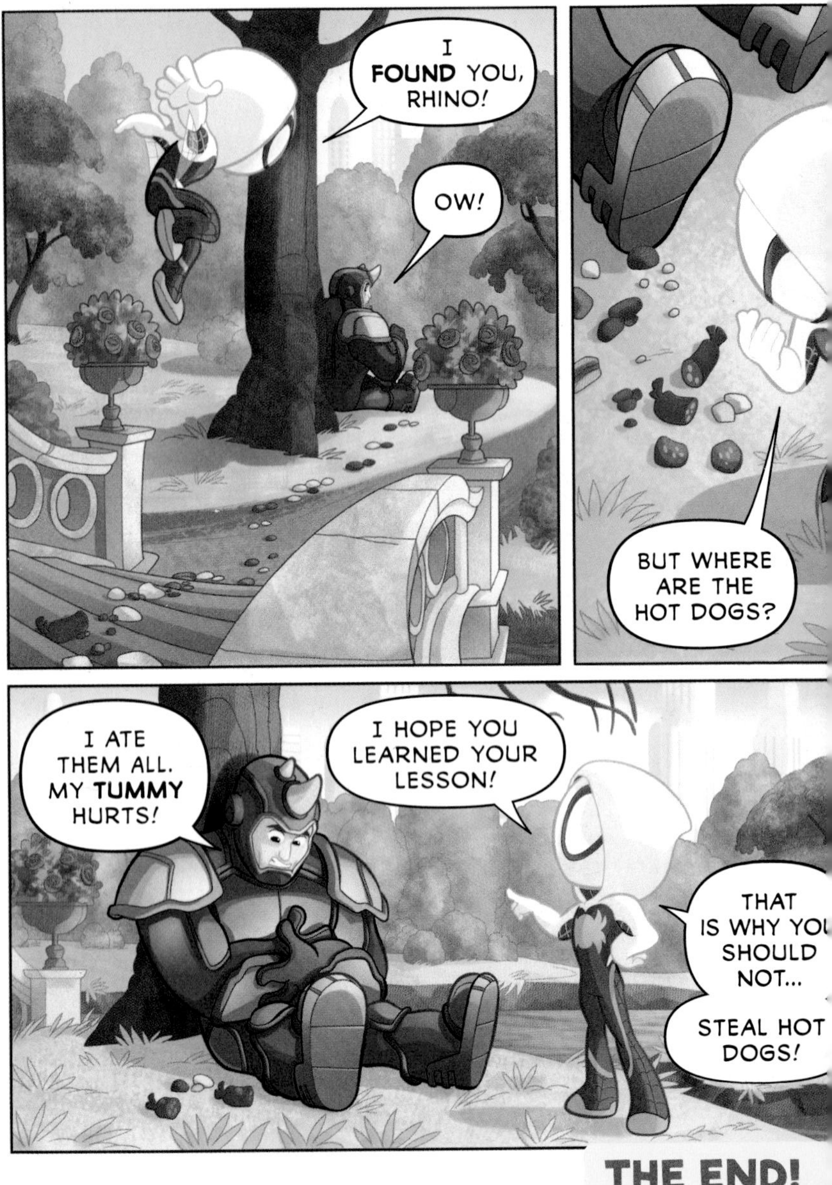
I FOUND YOU, RHINO!
OW!
BUT WHERE ARE THE HOT DOGS?
I ATE THEM ALL. MY TUMMY HURTS!
I HOPE YOU LEARNED YOUR LESSON!
THAT IS WHY YOU SHOULD NOT...
STEAL HOT DOGS!
THE END!

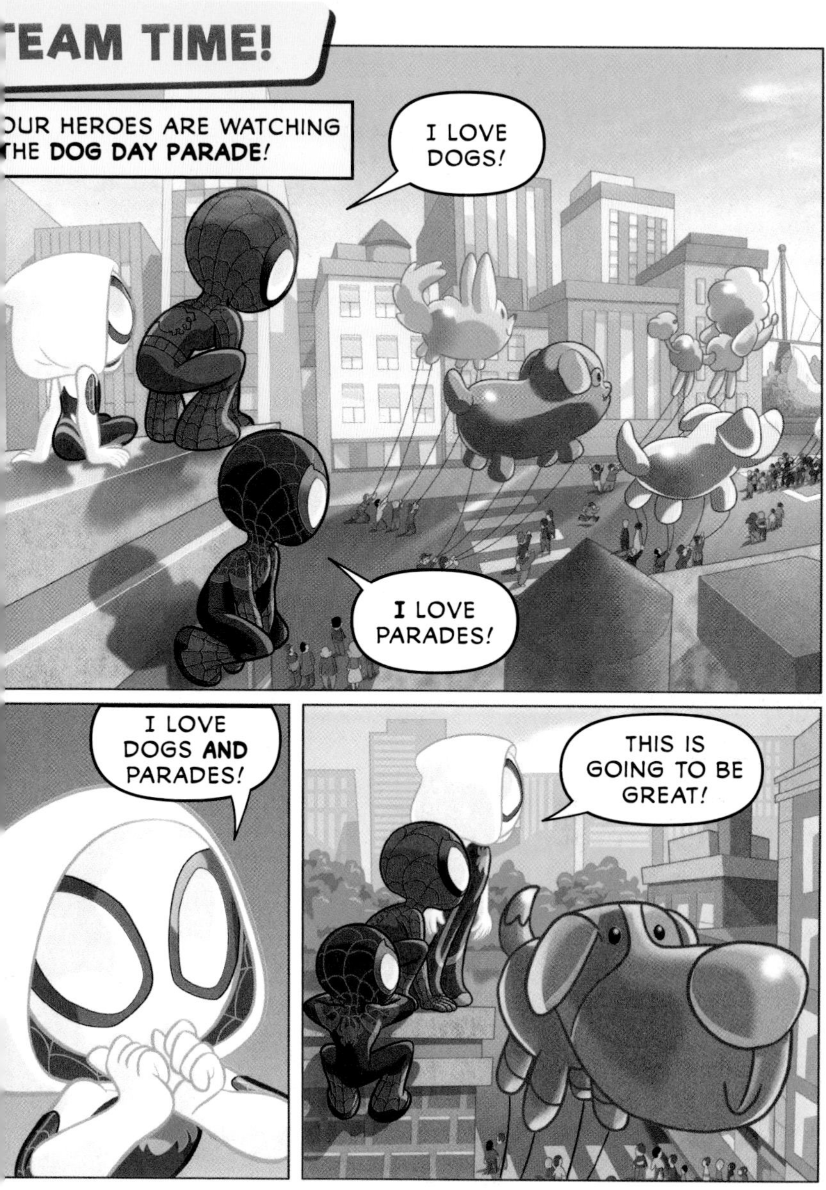
TEAM TIME!
OUR HEROES ARE WATCHING THE **DOG DAY PARADE**!
I LOVE DOGS!
I LOVE PARADES!
I LOVE DOGS **AND** PARADES!
THIS IS GOING TO BE GREAT!

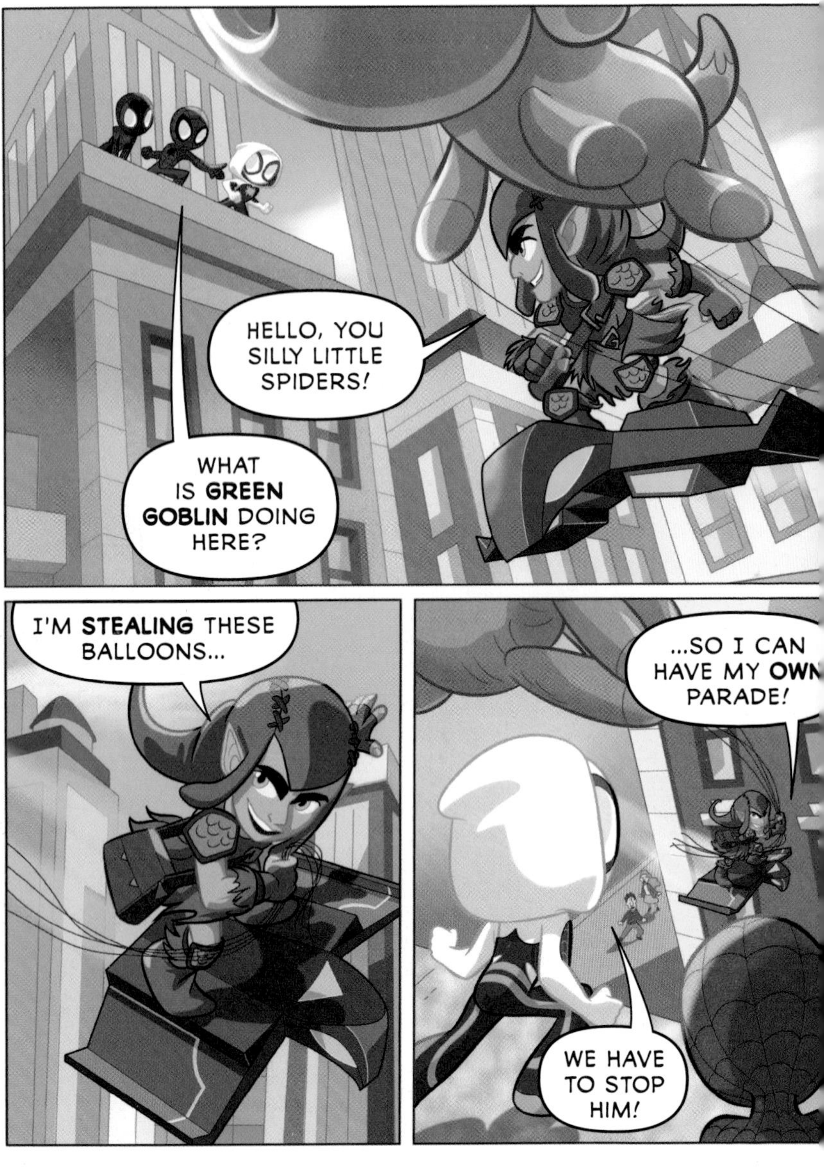

HELLO, YOU SILLY LITTLE SPIDERS!
WHAT IS GREEN GOBLIN DOING HERE?
I'M STEALING THESE BALLOONS...
...SO I CAN HAVE MY OWN PARADE!
WE HAVE TO STOP HIM!

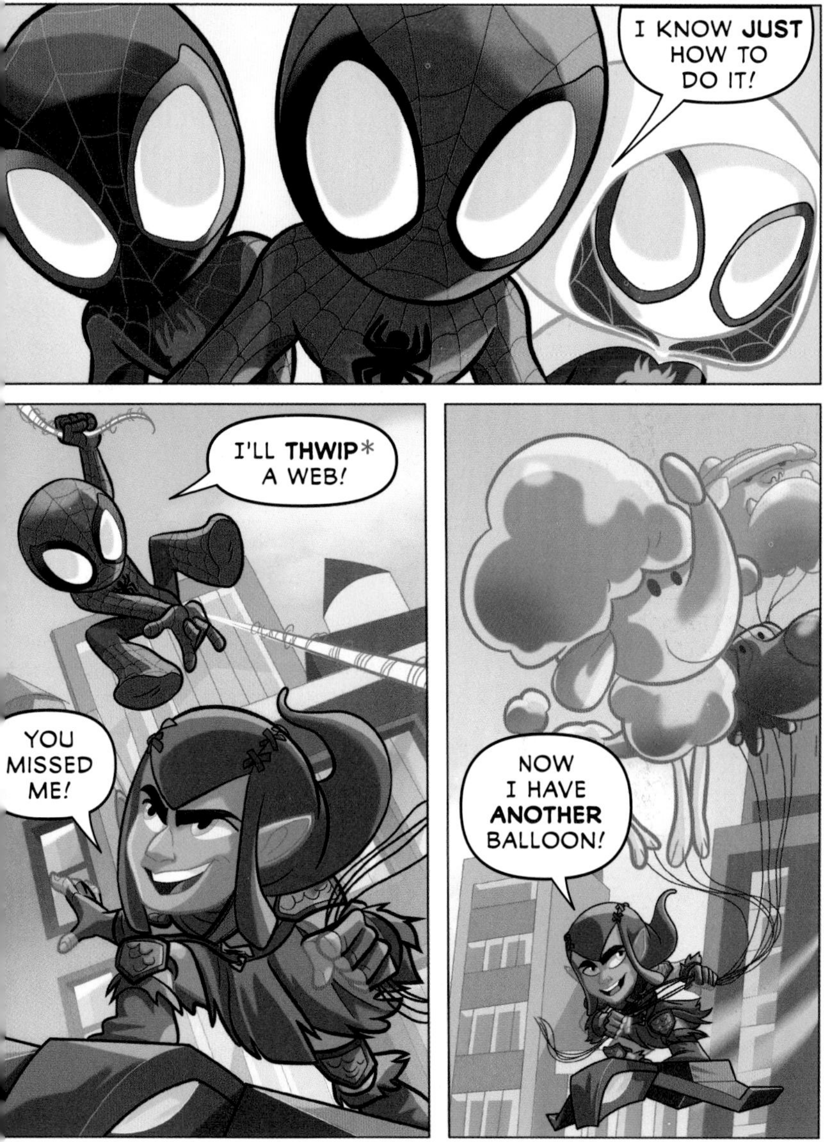
I KNOW **JUST** HOW TO DO IT!
I'LL **THWIP*** A WEB!
YOU MISSED ME!
NOW I HAVE **ANOTHER** BALLOON!

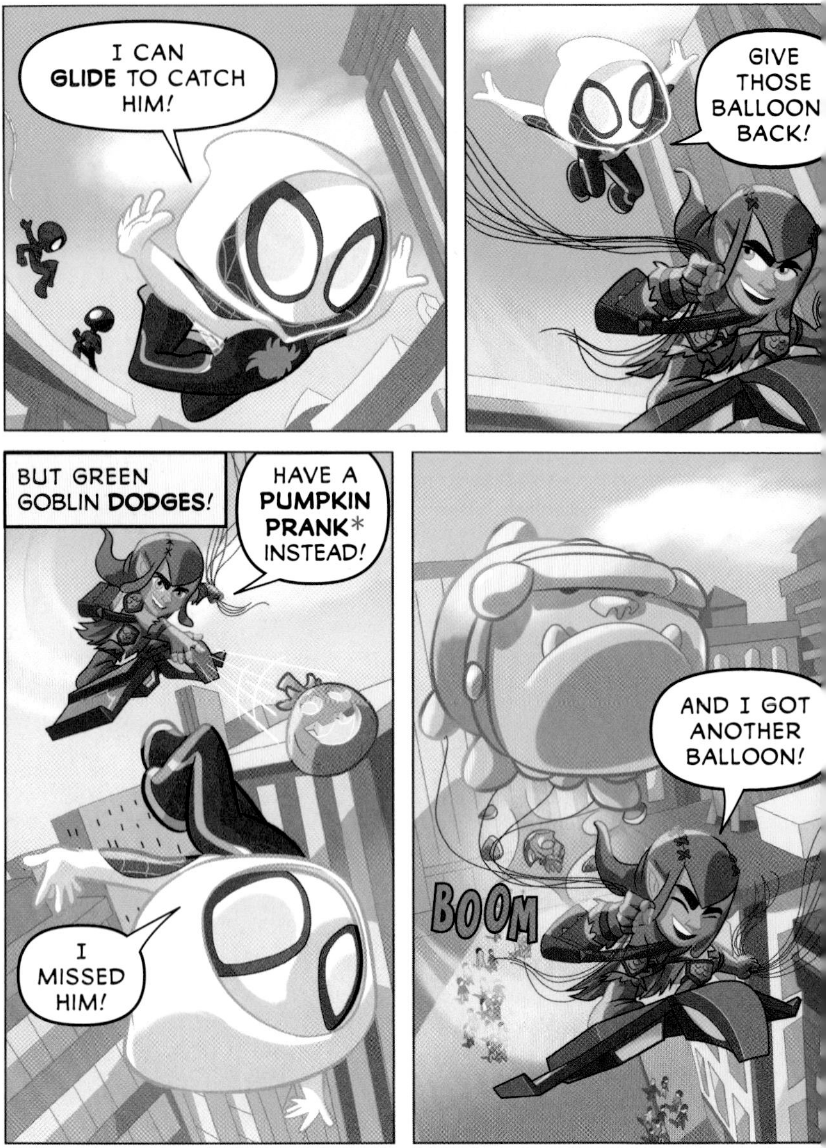
I CAN GLIDE TO CATCH HIM!
GIVE THOSE BALLOON BACK!
BUT GREEN GOBLIN DODGES!
HAVE A PUMPKIN PRANK* INSTEAD!
I MISSED HIM!
AND I GOT ANOTHER BALLOON!
BOOM

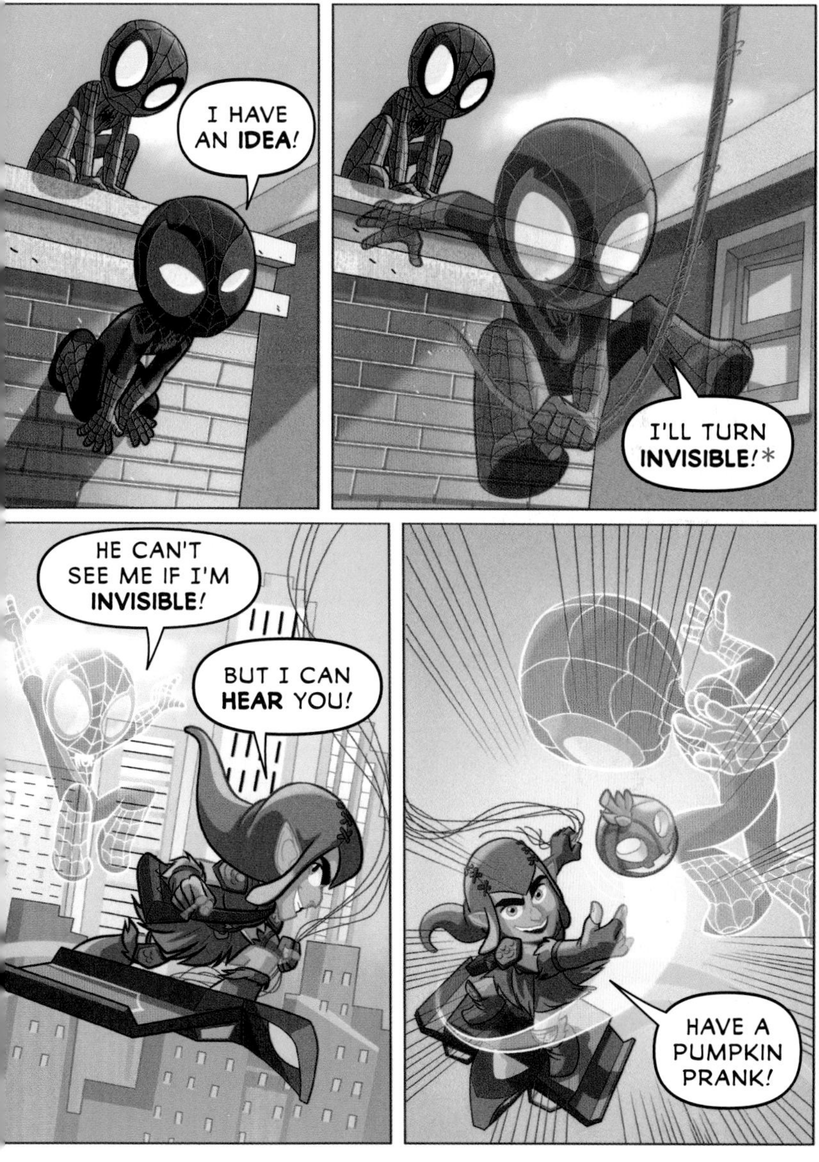
I HAVE AN **IDEA**!
I'LL TURN **INVISIBLE**!*
HE CAN'T SEE ME IF I'M **INVISIBLE**!
BUT I CAN **HEAR** YOU!
HAVE A PUMPKIN PRANK!

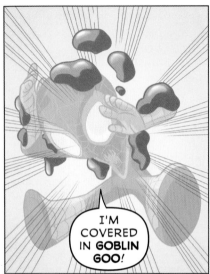

I'M COVERED IN **GOBLIN GOO**!

AND I HAVE **ANOTHER** BALLOON!

WHY CAN'T WE STOP HIM?

WHAT ARE WE DOING WRONG?

I KNOW!

WE DIDN'T WORK AS A **TEAM**!

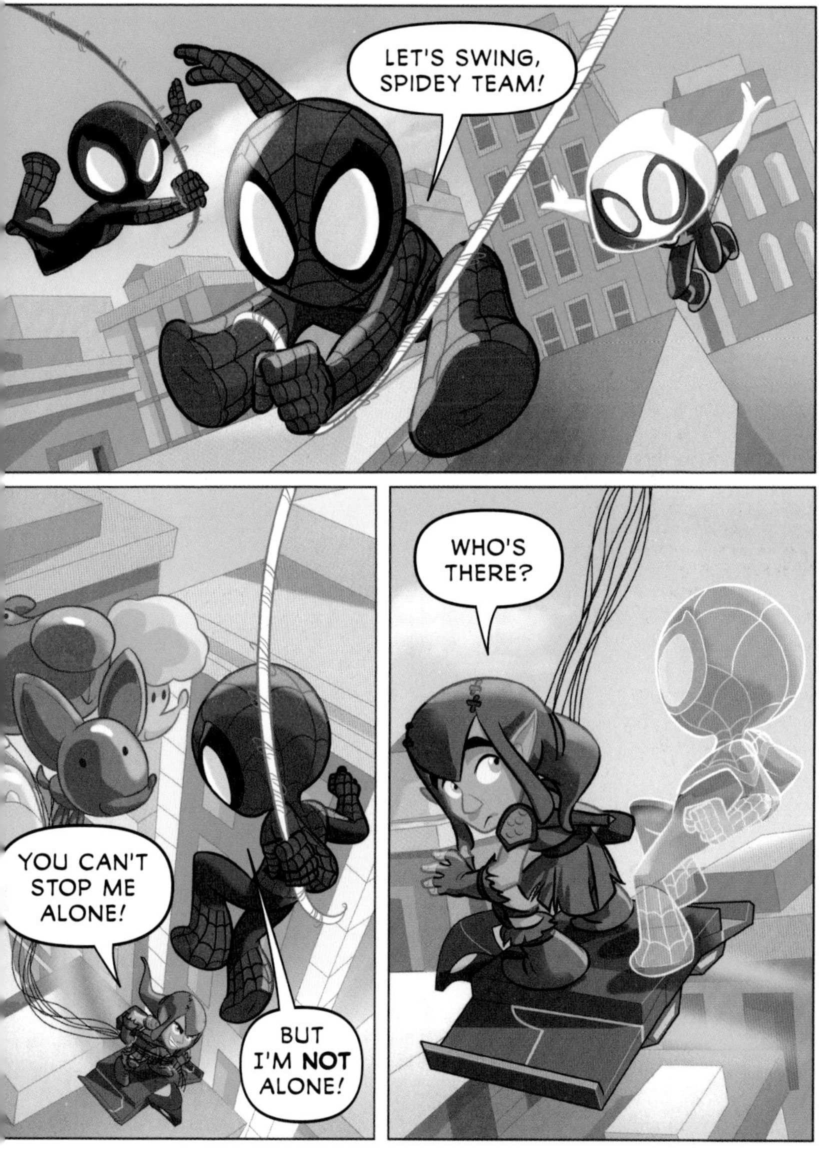
LET'S SWING, SPIDEY TEAM!
YOU CAN'T STOP ME ALONE!
BUT I'M **NOT** ALONE!
WHO'S THERE?

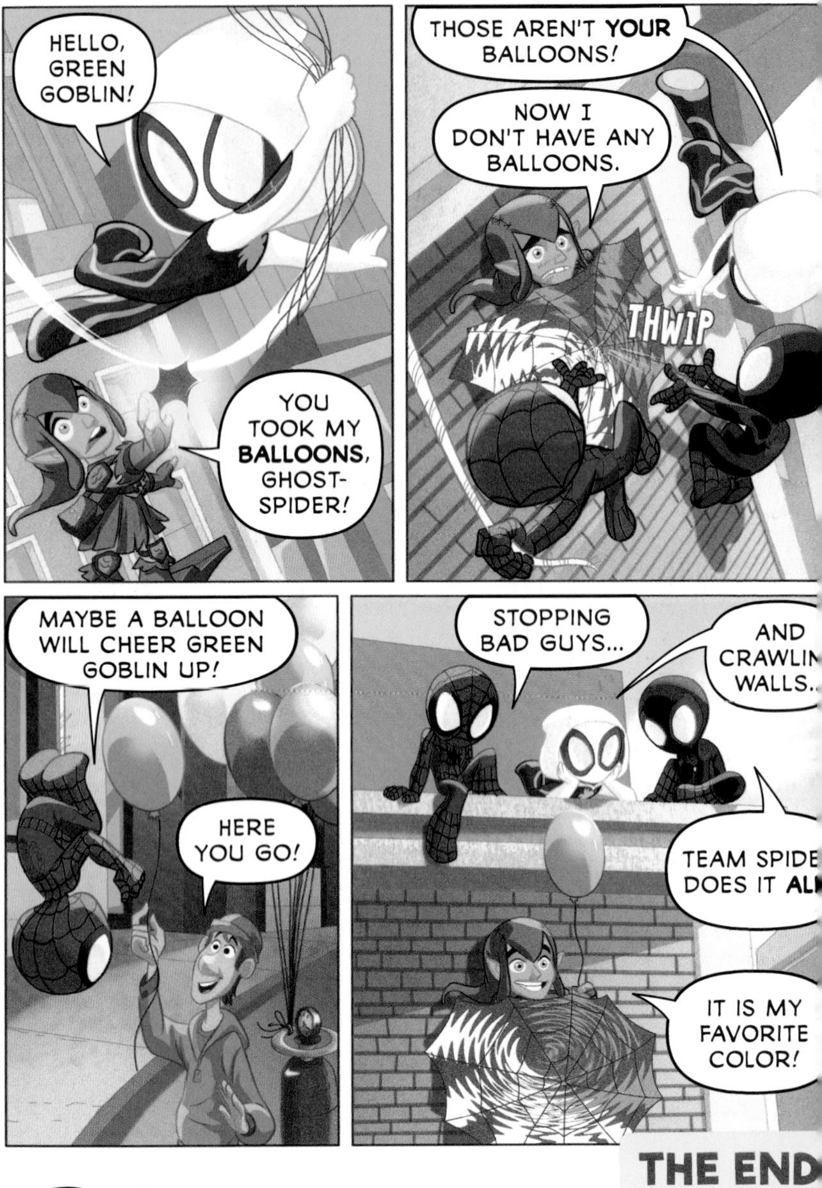
HELLO, GREEN GOBLIN!
YOU TOOK MY **BALLOONS**, GHOST-SPIDER!
THOSE AREN'T **YOUR** BALLOONS!
NOW I DON'T HAVE ANY BALLOONS.
THWIP
MAYBE A BALLOON WILL CHEER GREEN GOBLIN UP!
HERE YOU GO!
STOPPING BAD GUYS...
AND CRAWLIN WALLS..
TEAM SPIDE DOES IT AL
IT IS MY FAVORITE COLOR!
THE END

ND THE WINNER IS . . .

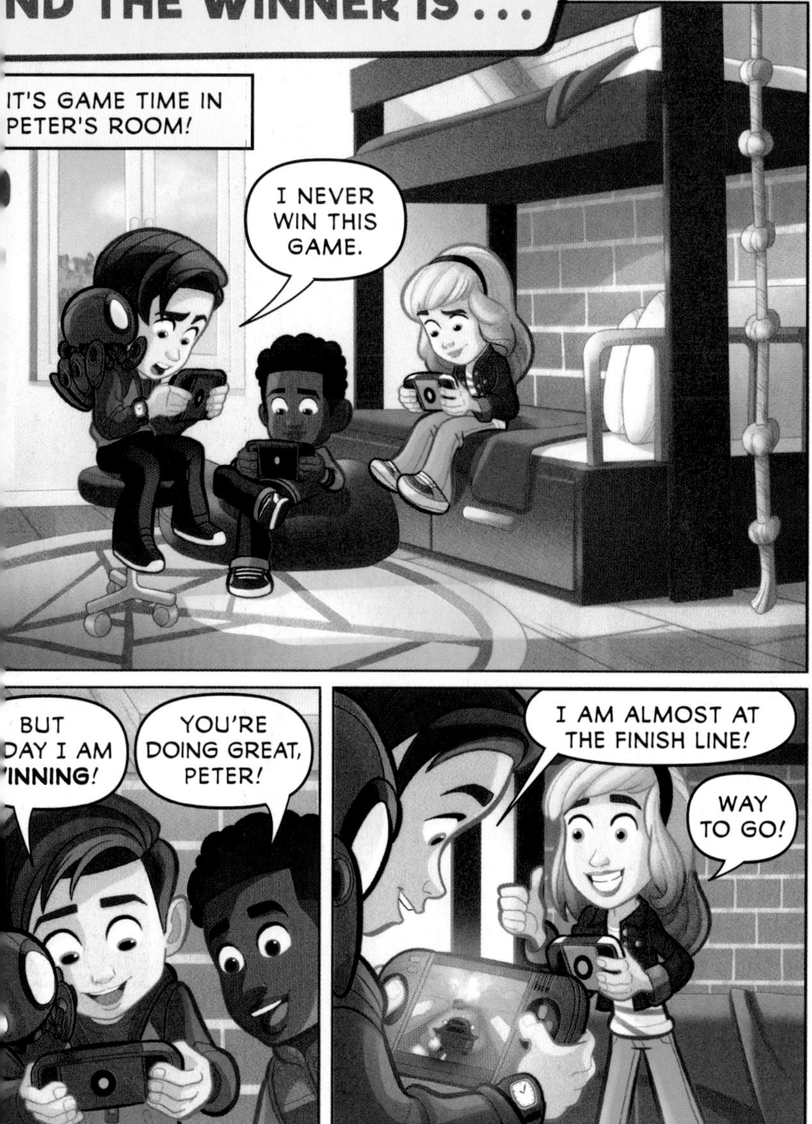
IT'S GAME TIME IN PETER'S ROOM!
I NEVER WIN THIS GAME.
BUT DAY I AM INNING!
YOU'RE DOING GREAT, PETER!
I AM ALMOST AT THE FINISH LINE!
WAY TO GO!

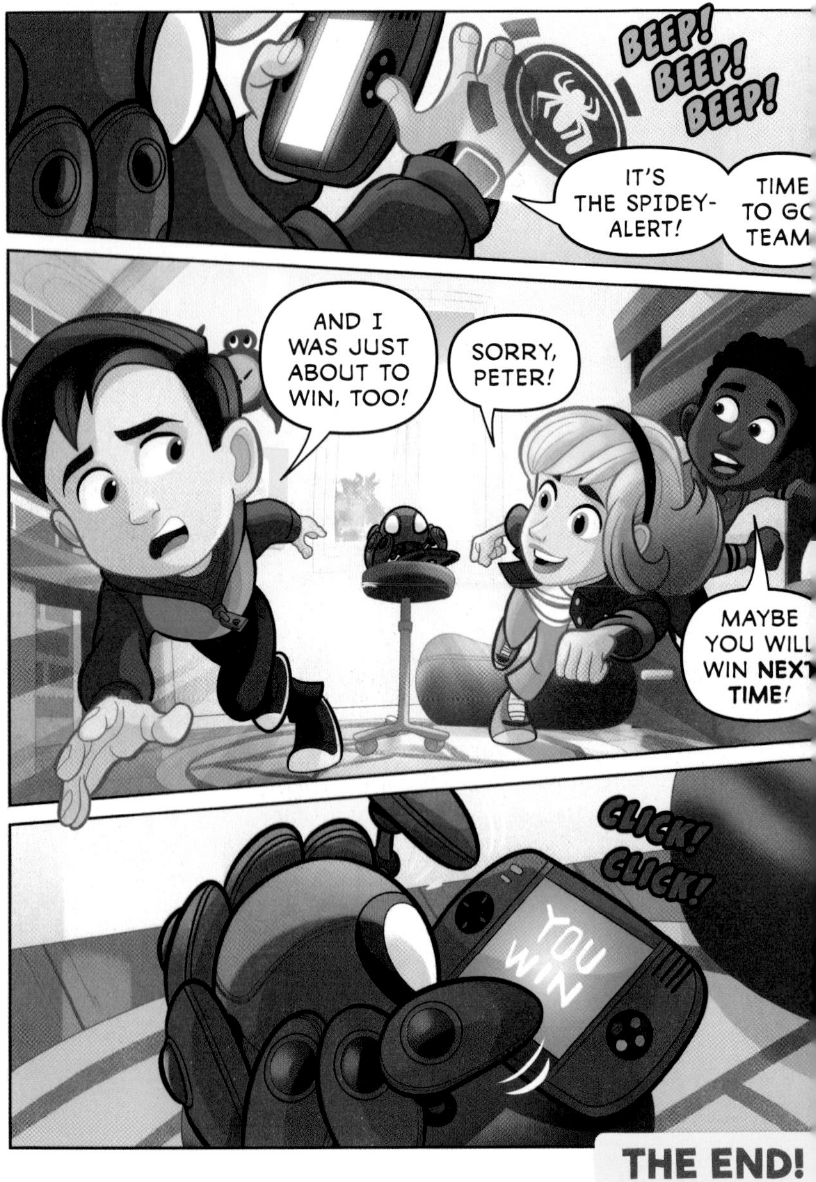
BEEP! BEEP! BEEP!
IT'S THE SPIDEY-ALERT!
TIME TO GO TEAM
AND I WAS JUST ABOUT TO WIN, TOO!
SORRY, PETER!
MAYBE YOU WILL WIN NEXT TIME!
CLICK! CLICK!
YOU WIN
THE END!

AGGING ALONG!

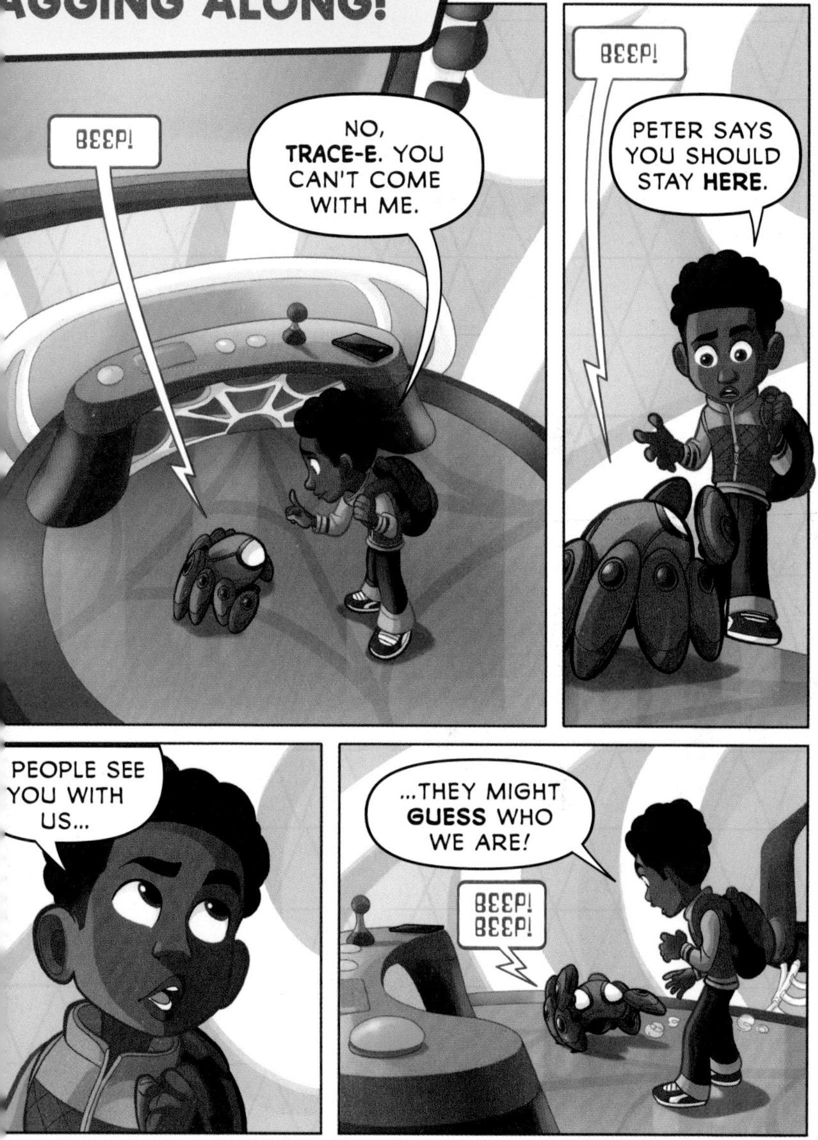

BEEP!
NO, TRACE-E. YOU CAN'T COME WITH ME.
BEEP!
PETER SAYS YOU SHOULD STAY HERE.
PEOPLE SEE YOU WITH US...
...THEY MIGHT GUESS WHO WE ARE!
BEEP! BEEP!

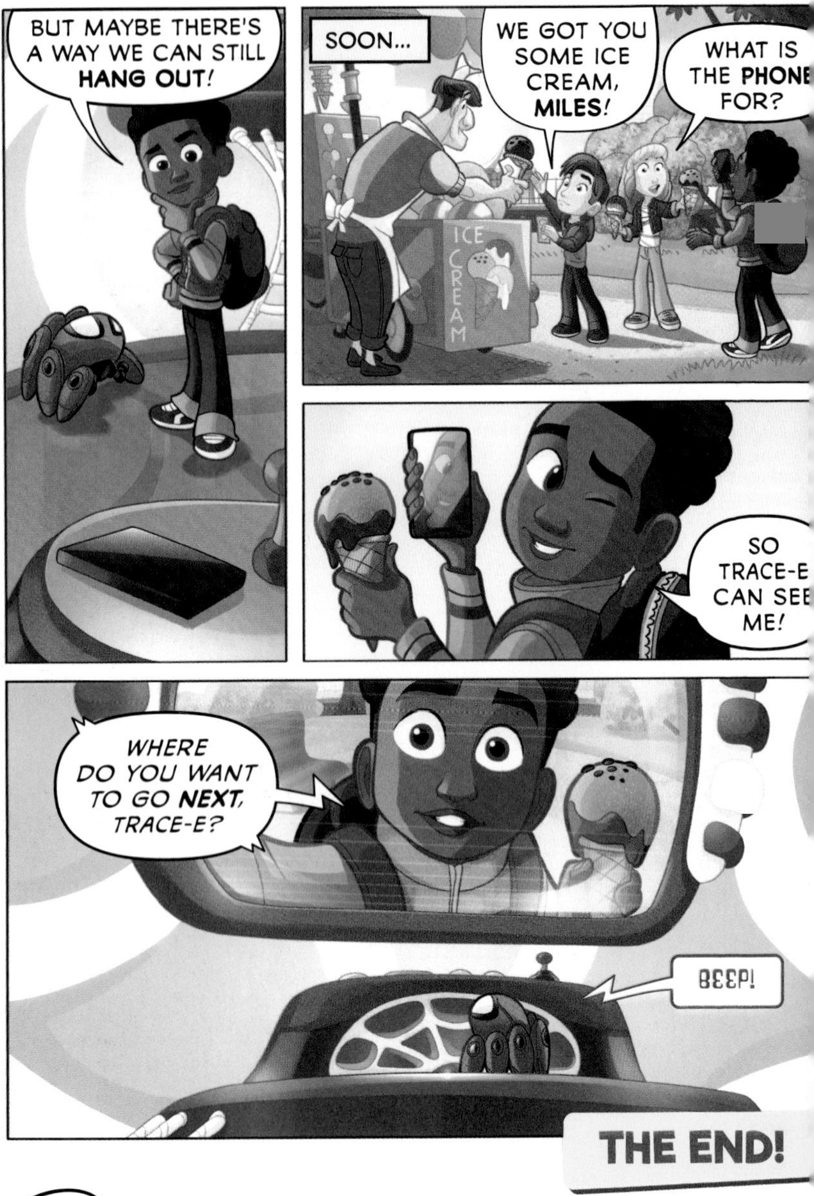
BUT MAYBE THERE'S A WAY WE CAN STILL **HANG OUT**!
SOON...
WE GOT YOU SOME ICE CREAM, **MILES**!
WHAT IS THE **PHONE** FOR?
ICE CREAM
SO TRACE-E CAN SEE ME!
*WHERE DO YOU WANT TO GO **NEXT**, TRACE-E?*
BEEP!
THE END!

NACK ATTACK!

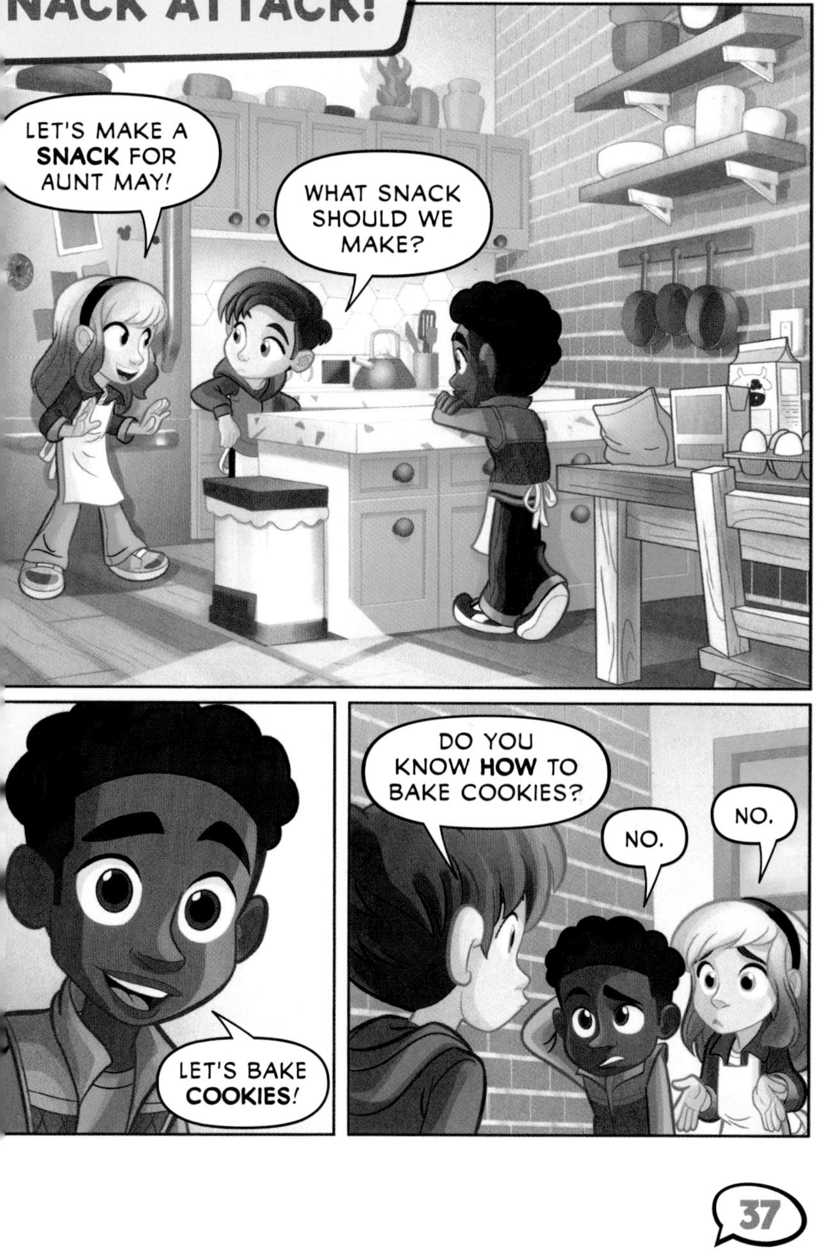
LET'S MAKE A **SNACK** FOR AUNT MAY!
WHAT SNACK SHOULD WE MAKE?
LET'S BAKE **COOKIES**!
DO YOU KNOW **HOW** TO BAKE COOKIES?
NO.
NO.

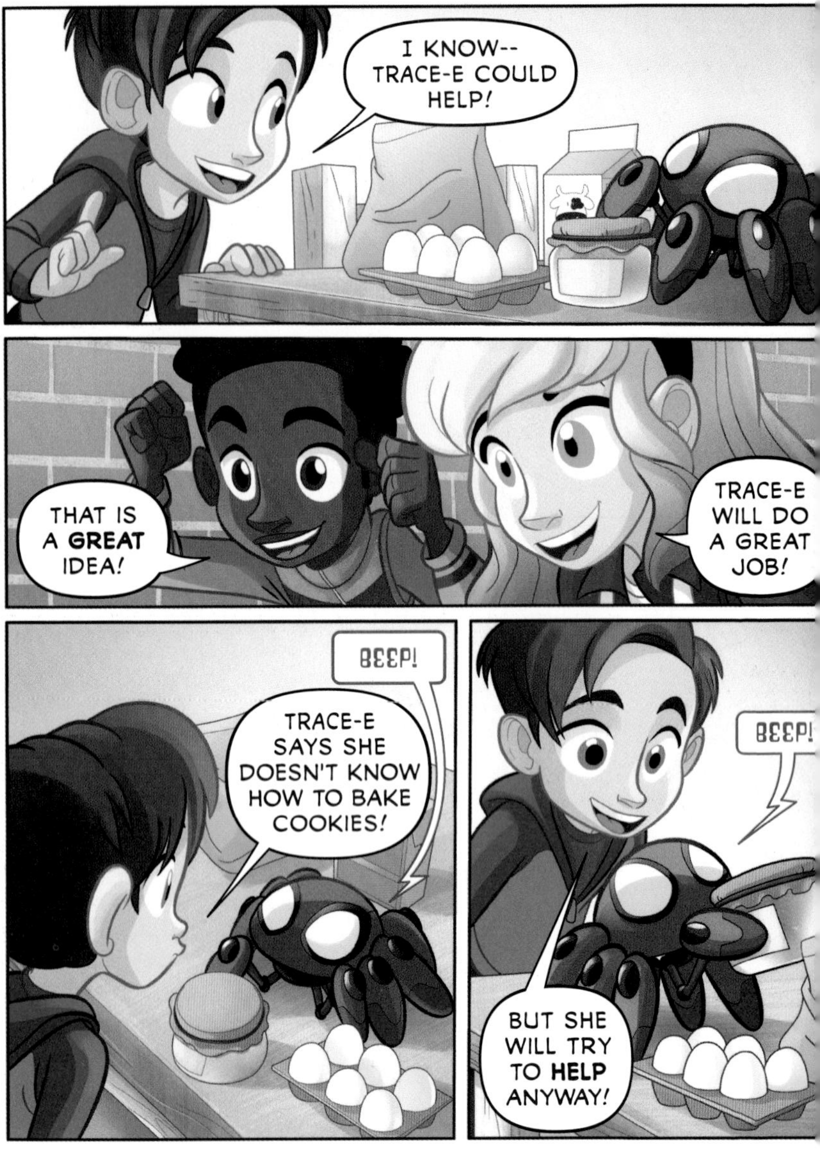
I KNOW--
TRACE-E COULD HELP!
THAT IS A **GREAT** IDEA!
TRACE-E WILL DO A GREAT JOB!
BEEP!
TRACE-E SAYS SHE DOESN'T KNOW HOW TO BAKE COOKIES!
BEEP!
BUT SHE WILL TRY TO **HELP** ANYWAY!

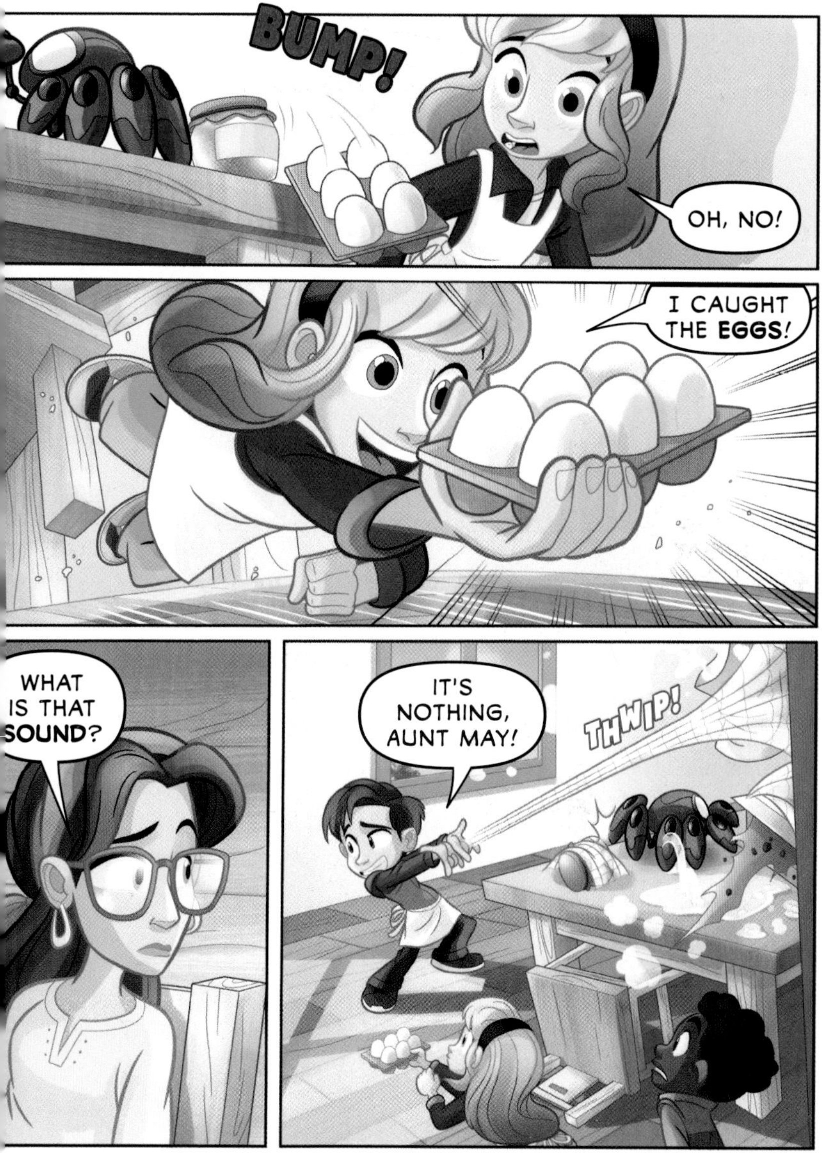
BUMP!
OH, NO!
I CAUGHT THE EGGS!
WHAT IS THAT SOUND?
IT'S NOTHING, AUNT MAY!
THWIP!

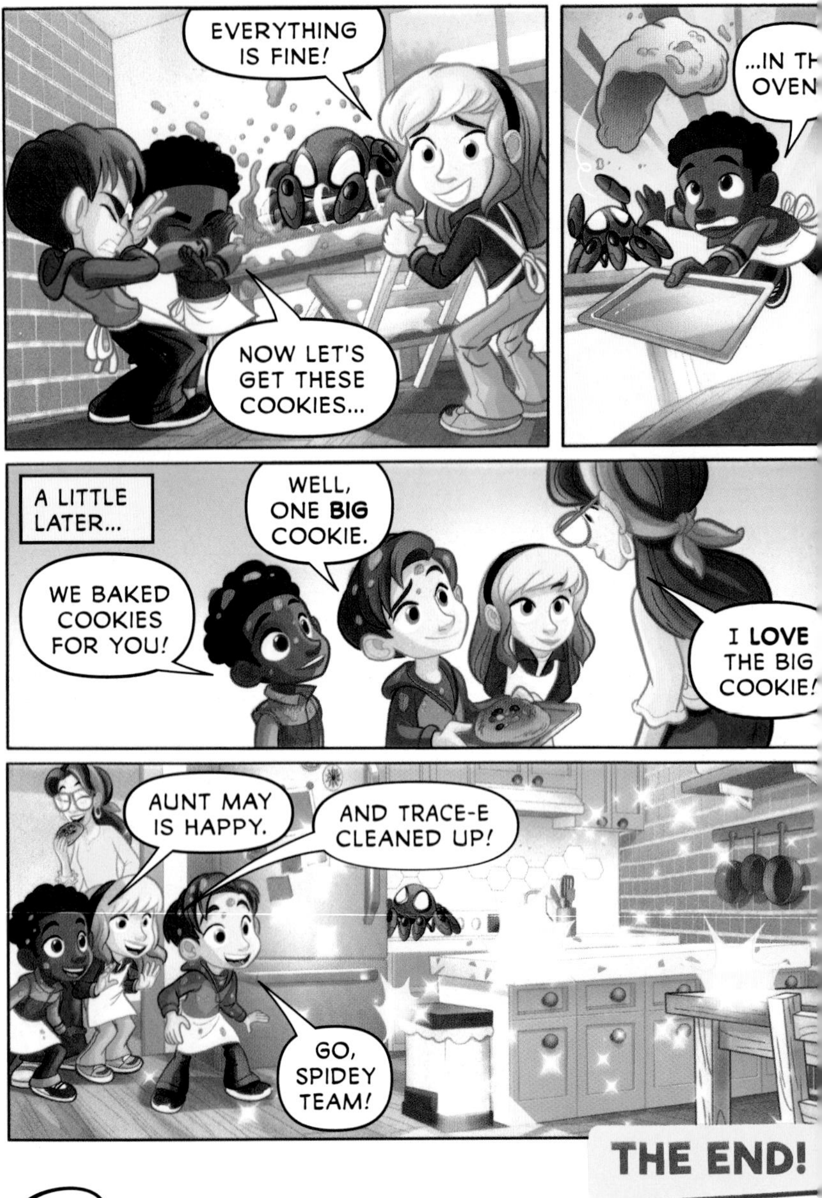
EVERYTHING IS FINE!
NOW LET'S GET THESE COOKIES...
...IN T
OVEN
A LITTLE LATER...
WE BAKED COOKIES FOR YOU!
WELL, ONE **BIG** COOKIE.
I **LOVE** THE BIG COOKIE!
AUNT MAY IS HAPPY.
AND TRACE-E CLEANED UP!
GO, SPIDEY TEAM!

THE END!

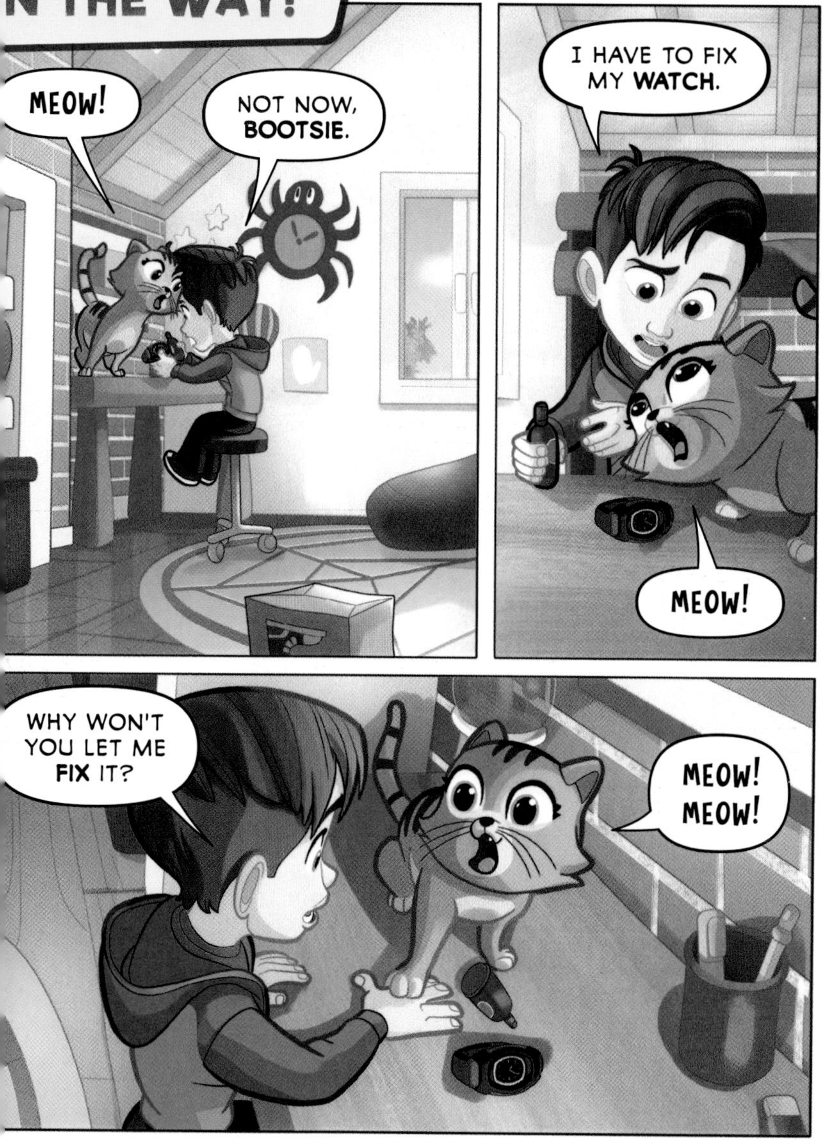
MEOW!
NOT NOW, BOOTSIE.
I HAVE TO FIX MY WATCH.
MEOW!
WHY WON'T YOU LET ME FIX IT?
MEOW! MEOW!

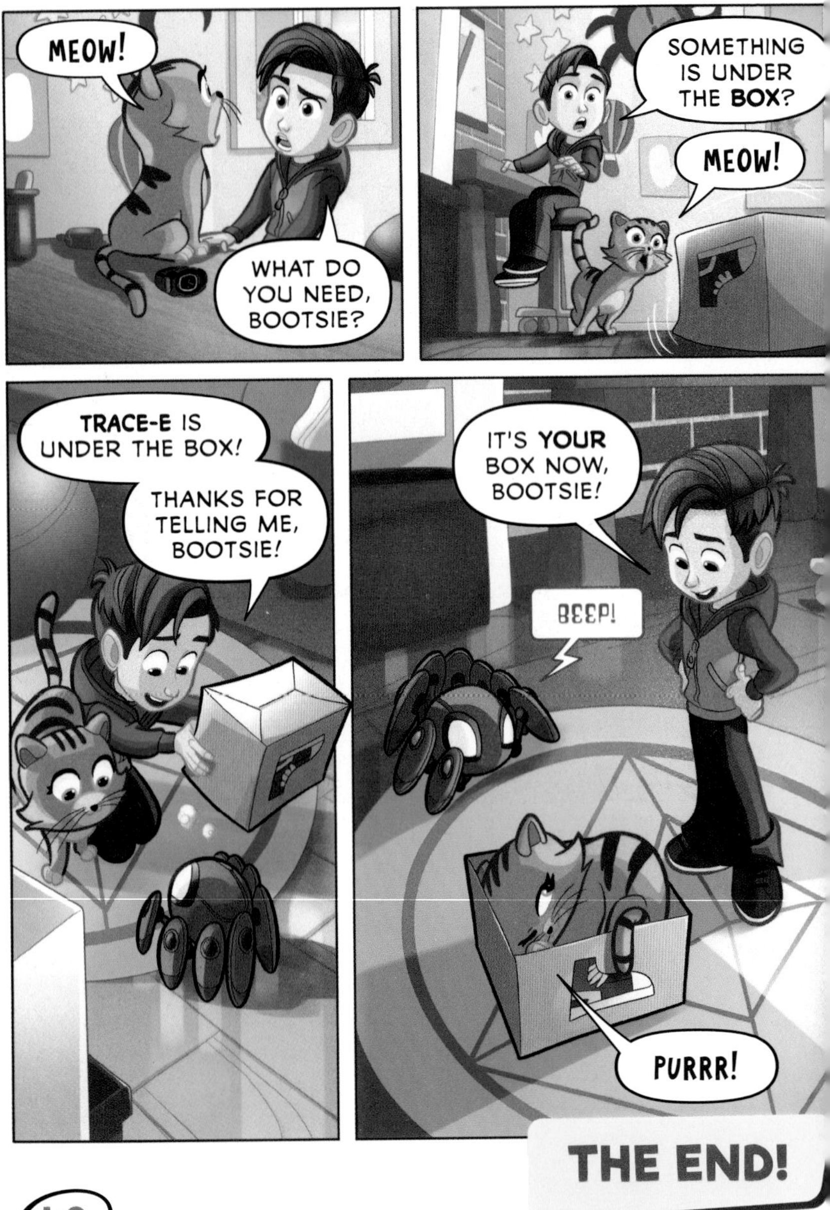
MEOW!
WHAT DO YOU NEED, BOOTSIE?
SOMETHING IS UNDER THE **BOX**?
MEOW!
TRACE-E IS UNDER THE BOX!
THANKS FOR TELLING ME, BOOTSIE!
IT'S **YOUR** BOX NOW, BOOTSIE!
BEEP!
PURRR!
THE END!

RHINO RACE!

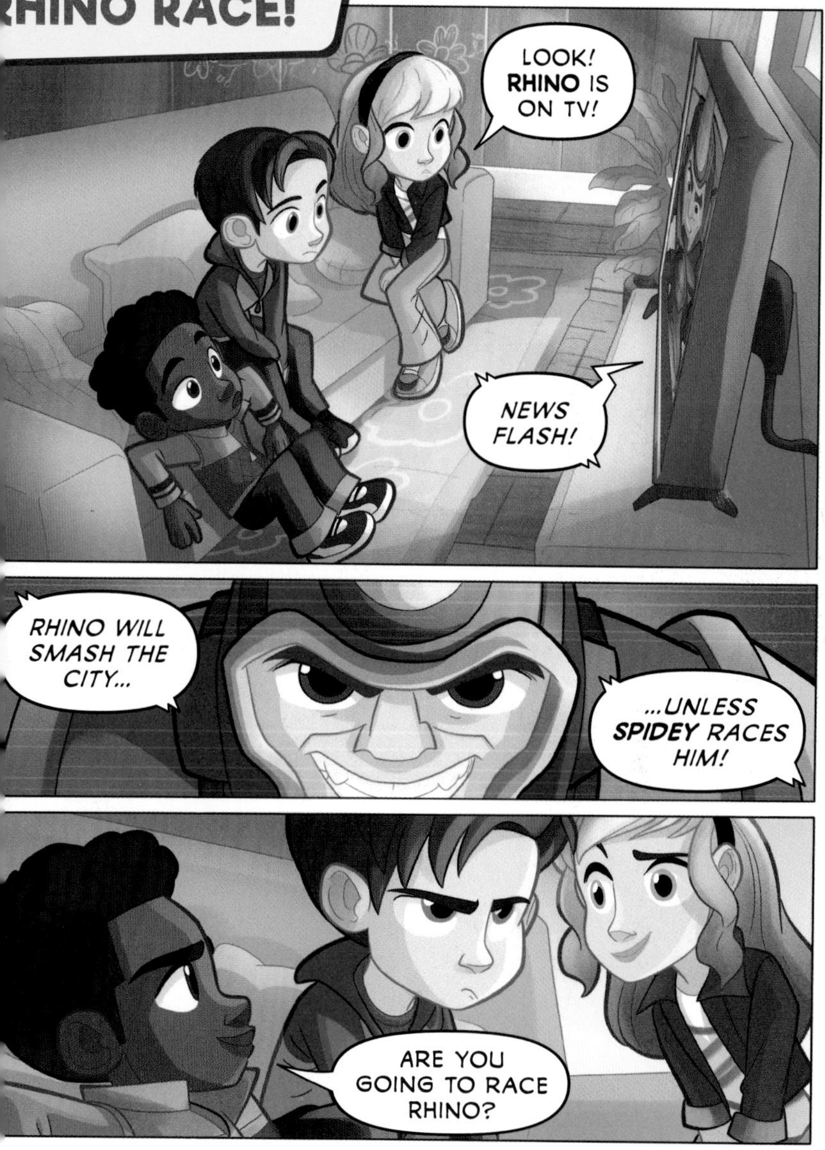
LOOK! **RHINO** IS ON TV!
NEWS FLASH!
RHINO WILL SMASH THE CITY...
*...UNLESS **SPIDEY** RACES HIM!*
ARE YOU GOING TO RACE RHINO?

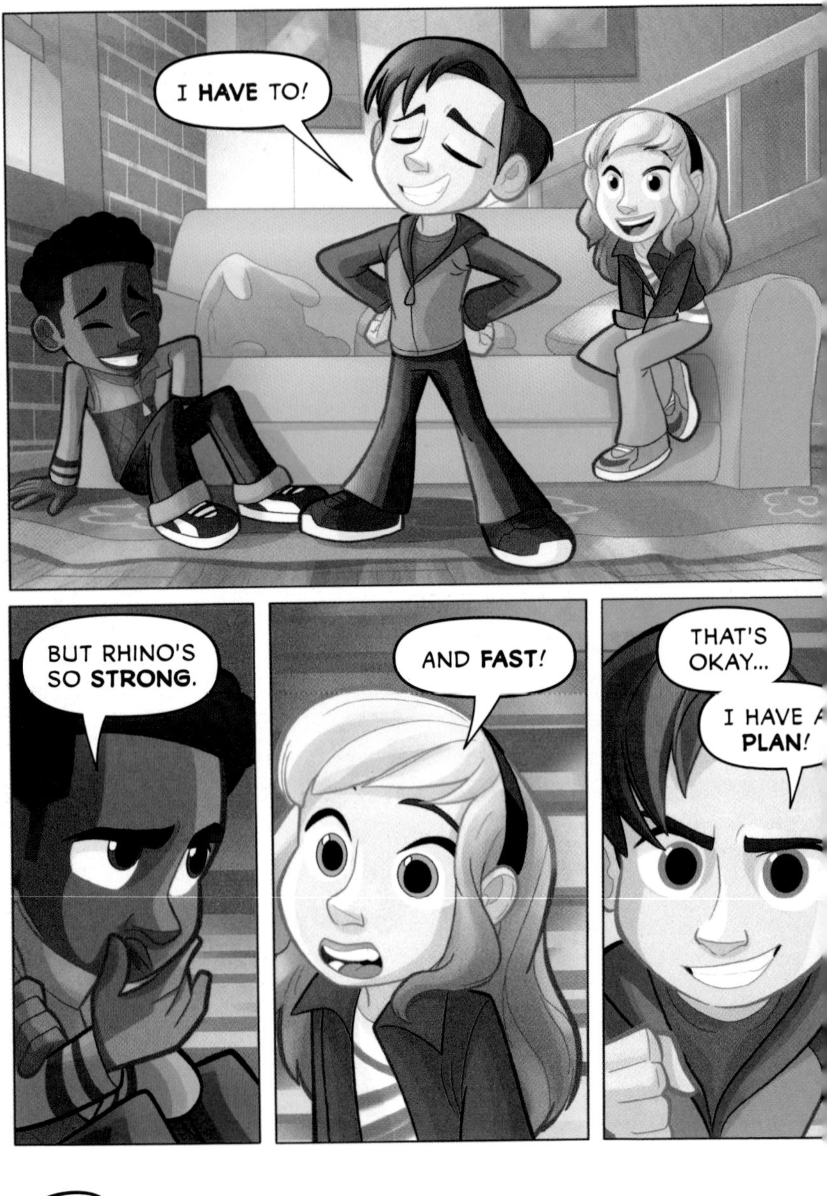
I HAVE TO!
BUT RHINO'S SO STRONG.
AND FAST!
THAT'S OKAY...
I HAVE A PLAN!

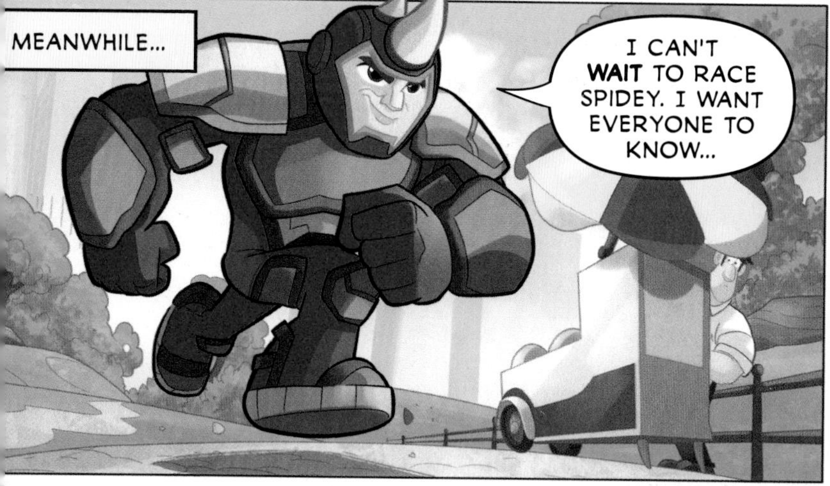
MEANWHILE...
I CAN'T WAIT TO RACE SPIDEY. I WANT EVERYONE TO KNOW...

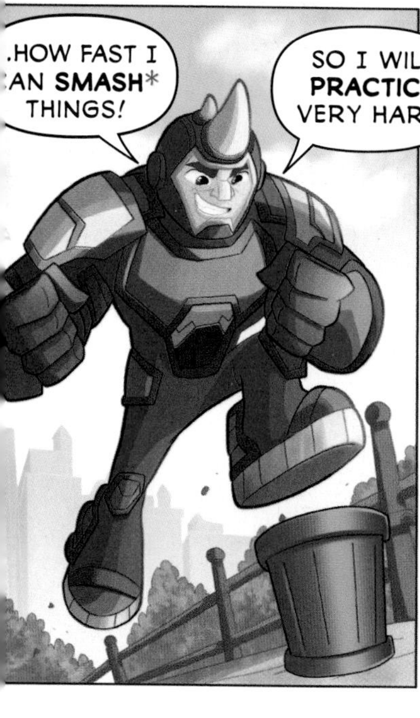
.HOW FAST I
AN SMASH* THINGS!
SO I WILL PRACTICE VERY HARD.

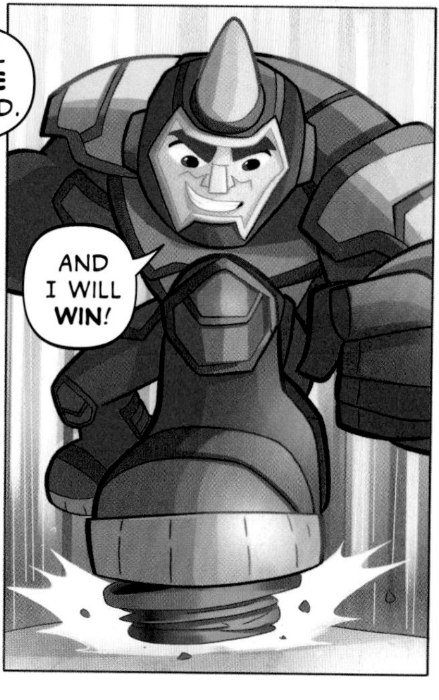
AND I WILL WIN!

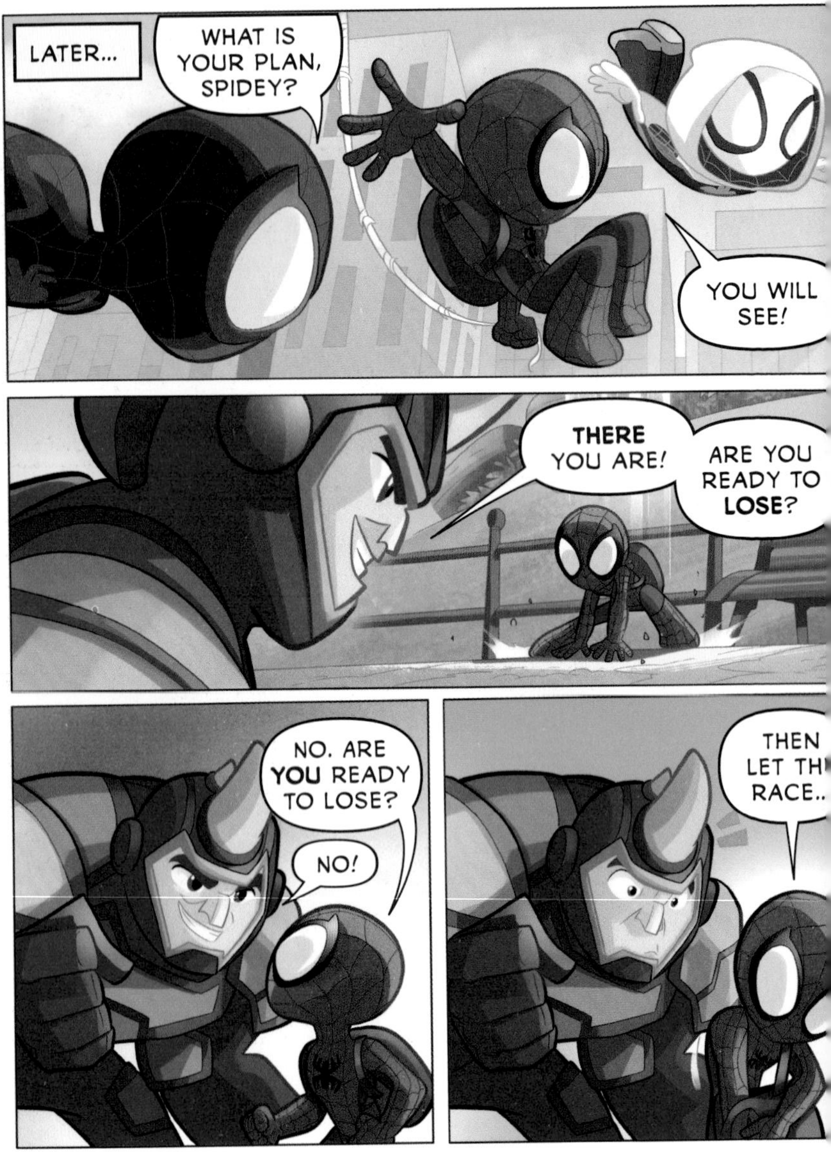
LATER...
WHAT IS YOUR PLAN, SPIDEY?
YOU WILL SEE!
THERE YOU ARE!
ARE YOU READY TO LOSE?
NO. ARE YOU READY TO LOSE?
NO!
THEN LET TH
RACE..

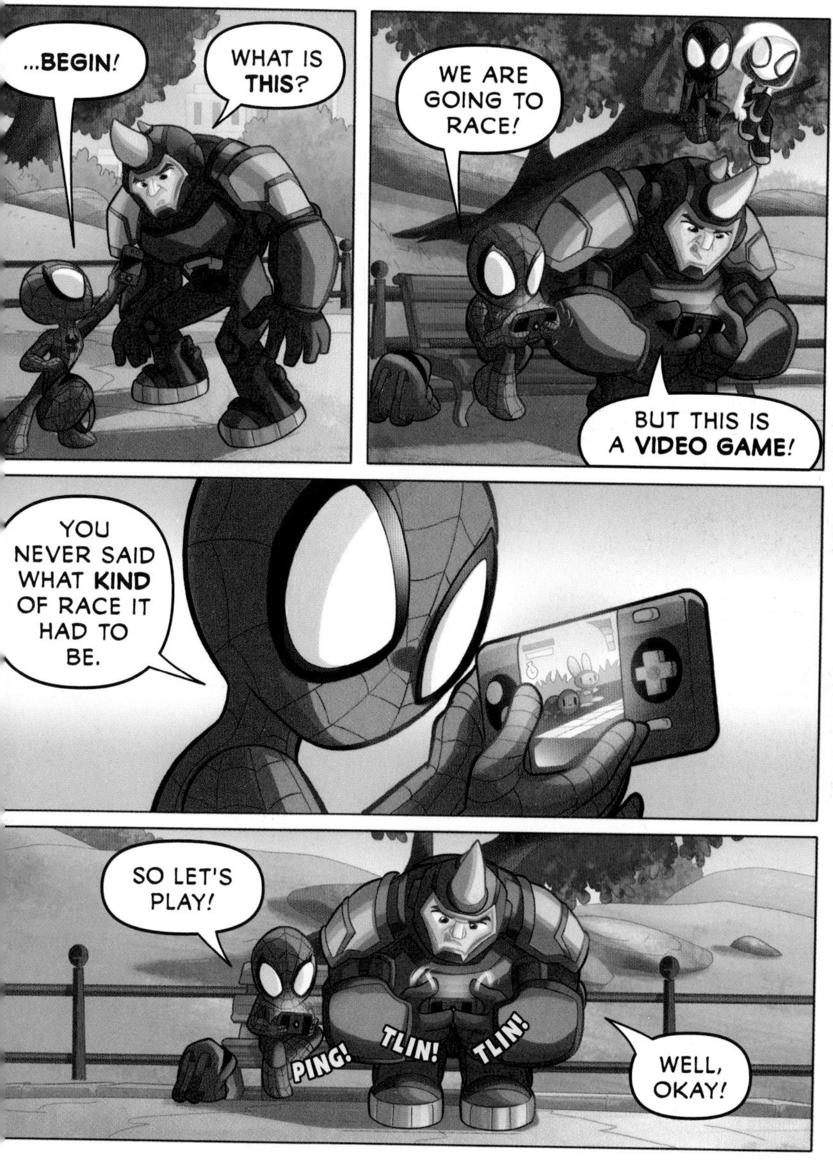
...BEGIN!
WHAT IS THIS?
WE ARE GOING TO RACE!
BUT THIS IS A VIDEO GAME!
YOU NEVER SAID WHAT KIND OF RACE IT HAD TO BE.
SO LET'S PLAY!
PING!
TLIN!
TLIN!
WELL, OKAY!

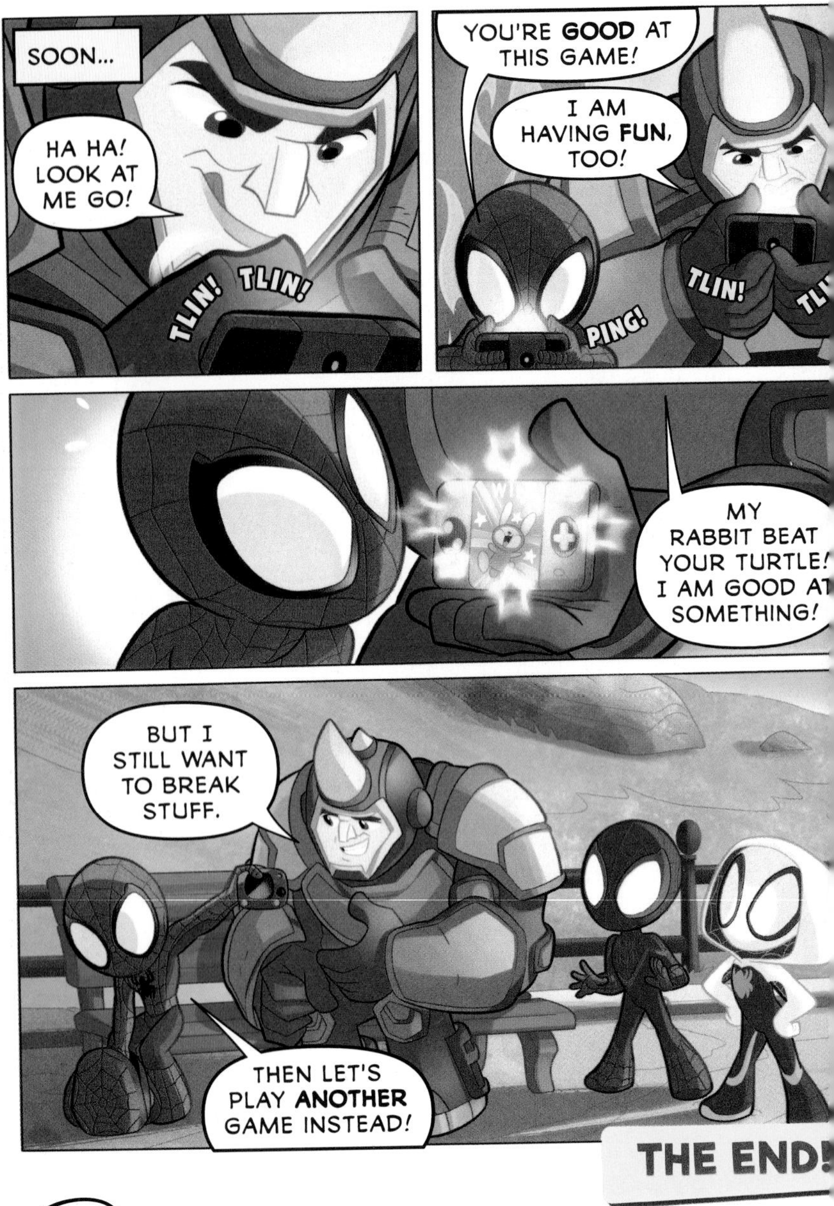
SOON...
HA HA! LOOK AT ME GO!
TLIN! TLIN!
YOU'RE **GOOD** AT THIS GAME!
I AM HAVING **FUN**, TOO!
TLIN!
PING!
MY RABBIT BEAT YOUR TURTLE! I AM GOOD AT SOMETHING!
BUT I STILL WANT TO BREAK STUFF.
THEN LET'S PLAY **ANOTHER** GAME INSTEAD!
THE END!

THE BIG LIBRARY PRANK

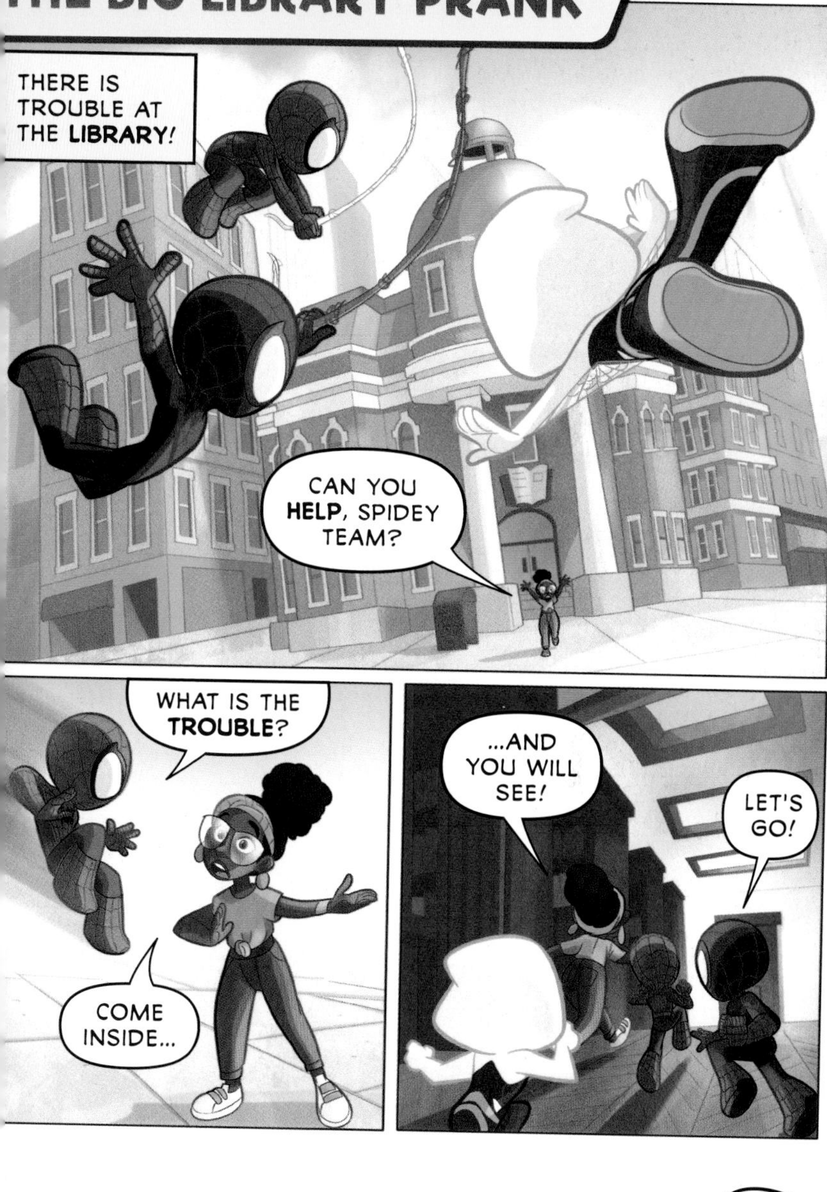
THERE IS TROUBLE AT THE **LIBRARY**!
CAN YOU **HELP**, SPIDEY TEAM?
WHAT IS THE **TROUBLE**?
COME INSIDE...
...AND YOU WILL SEE!
LET'S GO!

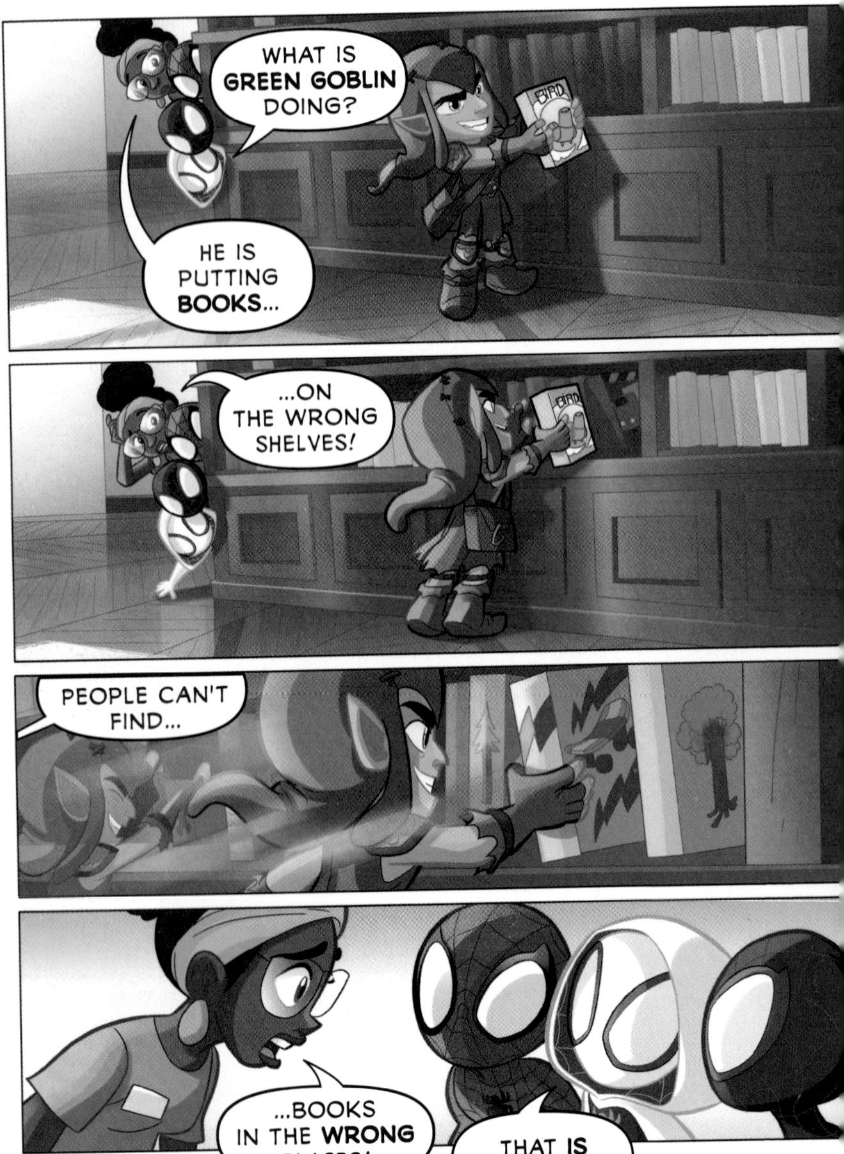
WHAT IS **GREEN GOBLIN** DOING?
BIRD
HE IS PUTTING **BOOKS**...
...ON THE WRONG SHELVES!
BIRD
PEOPLE CAN'T FIND...
...BOOKS IN THE **WRONG** PLACES!
THAT **IS** TROUBLE!

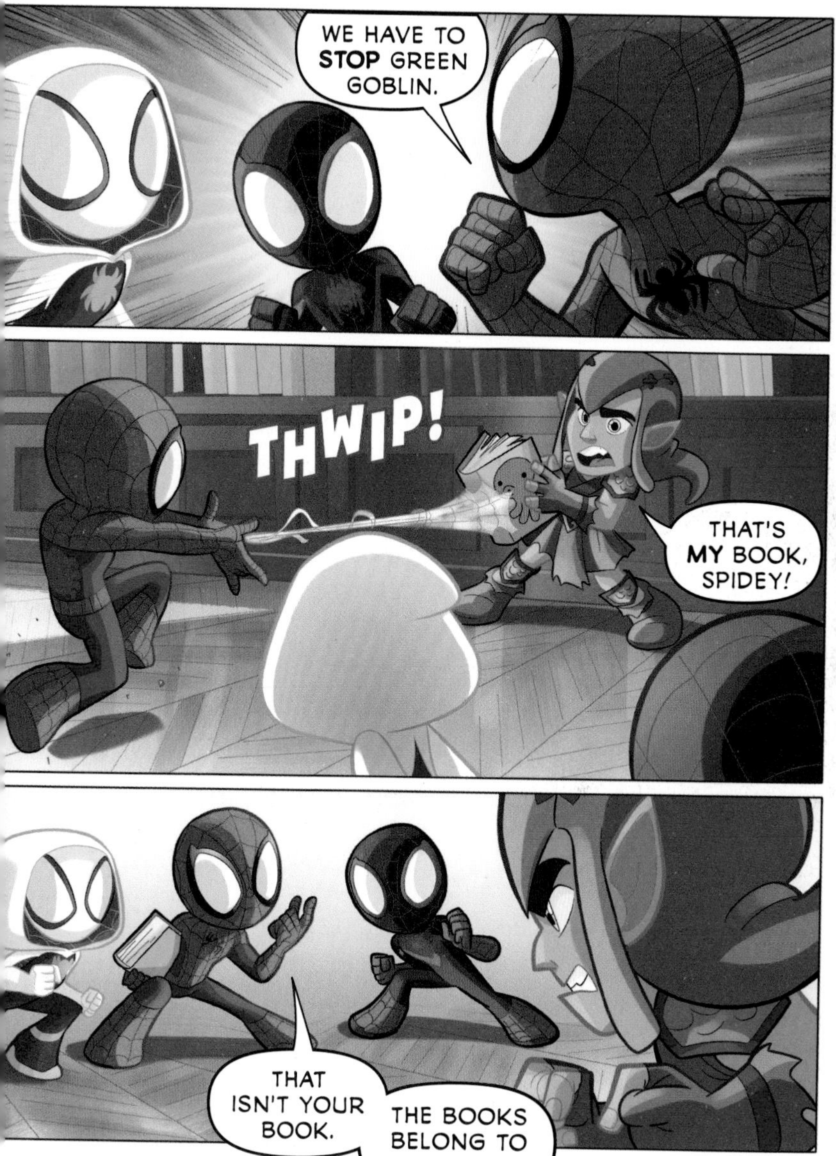
WE HAVE TO STOP GREEN GOBLIN.
THWIP!
THAT'S MY BOOK, SPIDEY!
THAT ISN'T YOUR BOOK.
THE BOOKS BELONG TO EVERYONE!

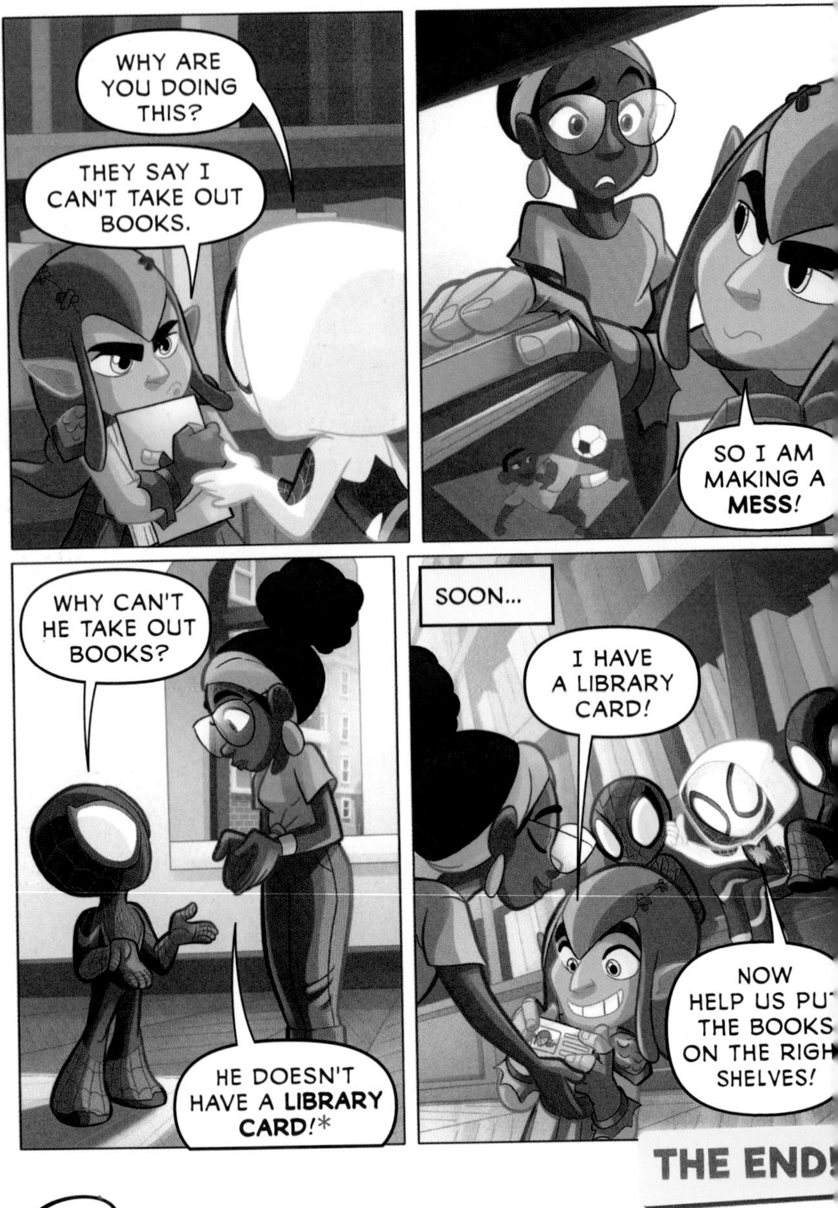

WHY ARE YOU DOING THIS?
THEY SAY I CAN'T TAKE OUT BOOKS.
SO I AM MAKING A **MESS**!
WHY CAN'T HE TAKE OUT BOOKS?
HE DOESN'T HAVE A **LIBRARY CARD**!*
SOON...
I HAVE A LIBRARY CARD!
NOW HELP US PU THE BOOKS ON THE RIGH SHELVES!
THE END!

MEET BLACK PANTHER!

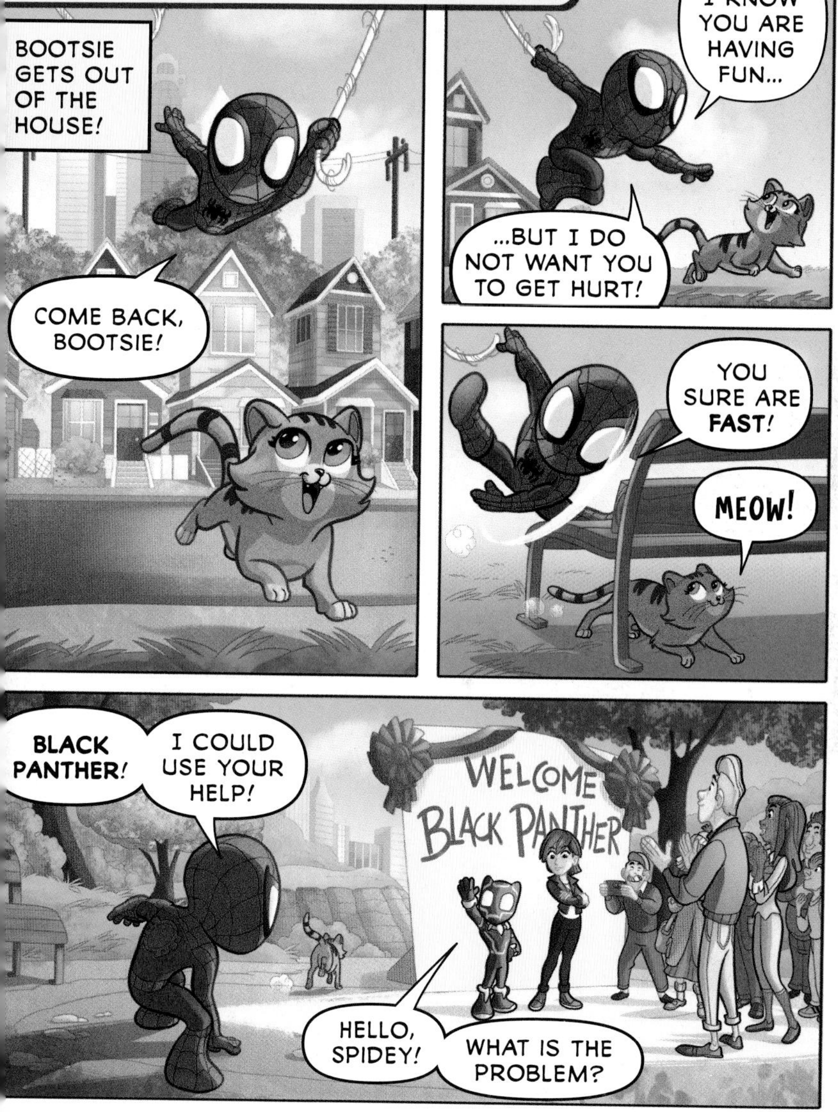
BOOTSIE GETS OUT OF THE HOUSE!
COME BACK, BOOTSIE!
I KNOW YOU ARE HAVING FUN...
...BUT I DO NOT WANT YOU TO GET HURT!
YOU SURE ARE **FAST**!
MEOW!
BLACK PANTHER!
I COULD USE YOUR HELP!
WELCOME BLACK PANTHER
HELLO, SPIDEY!
WHAT IS THE PROBLEM?

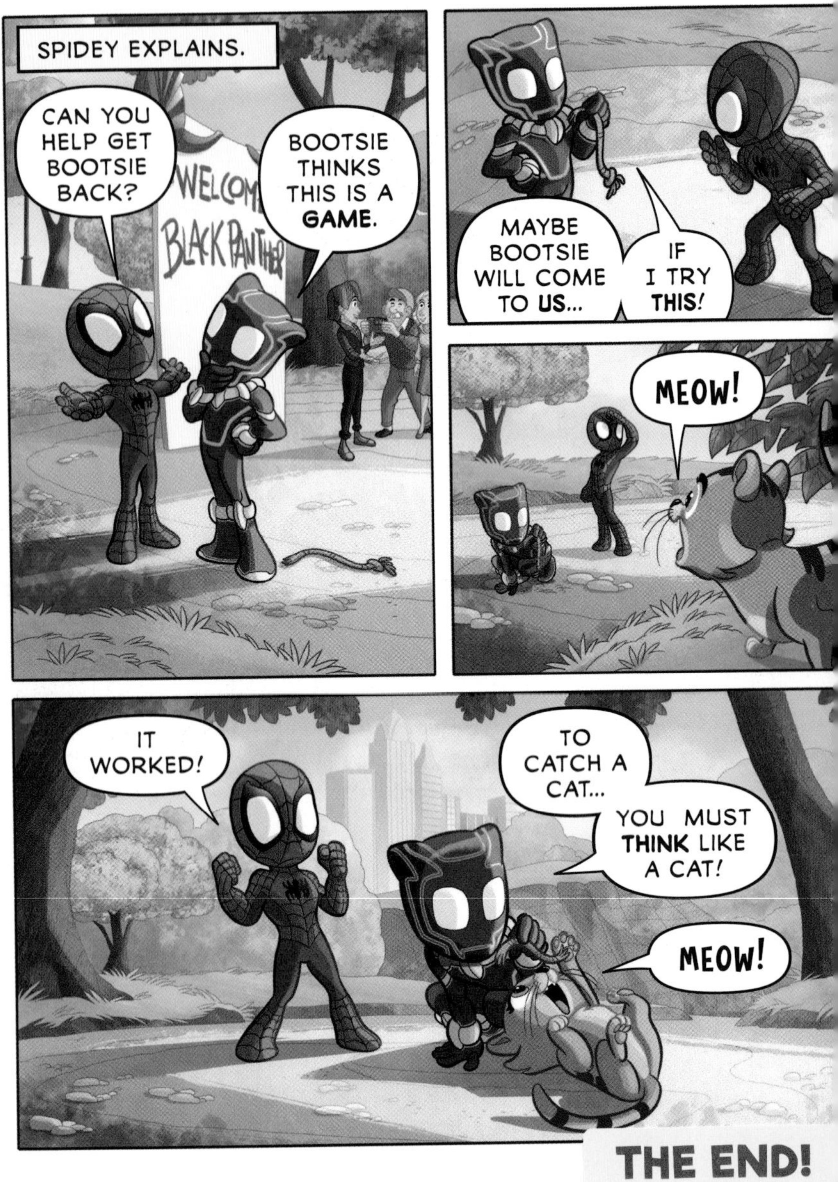
SPIDEY EXPLAINS.
CAN YOU HELP GET BOOTSIE BACK?
BOOTSIE THINKS THIS IS A **GAME**.
MAYBE BOOTSIE WILL COME TO **US**...
IF I TRY **THIS**!
MEOW!
IT WORKED!
TO CATCH A CAT...
YOU MUST **THINK** LIKE A CAT!
MEOW!
THE END!

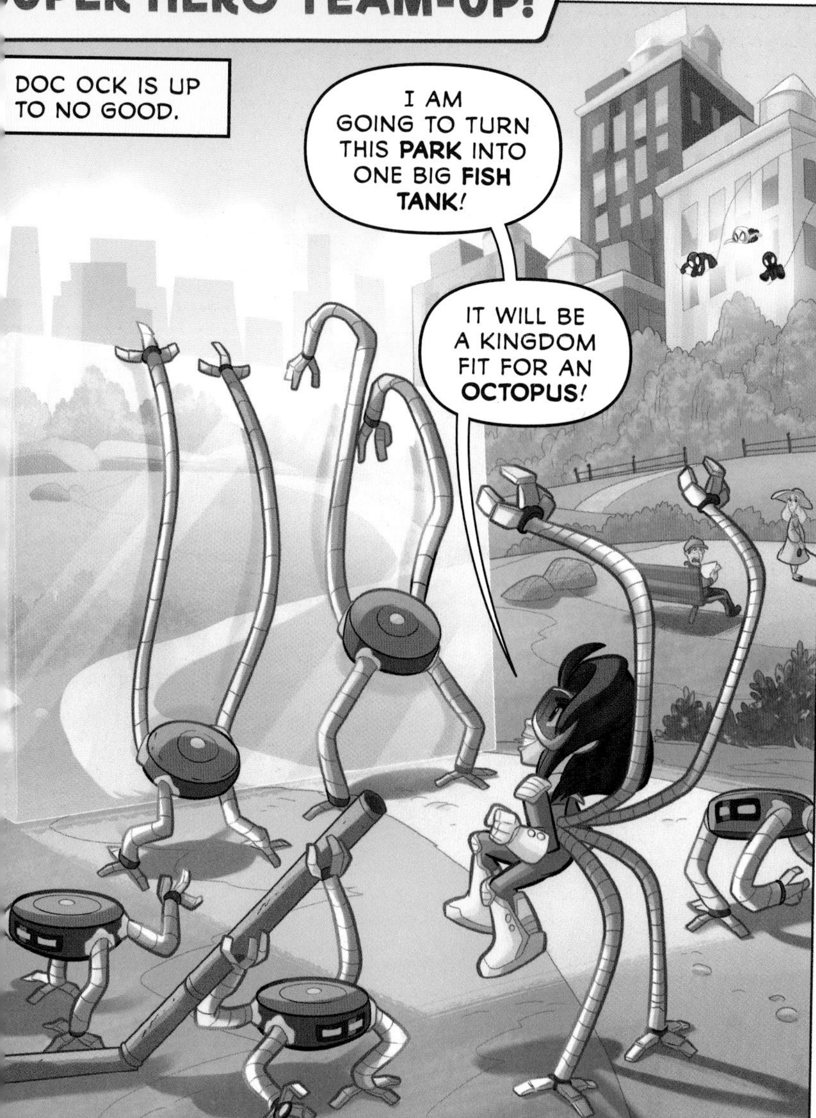
DOC OCK IS UP TO NO GOOD.
I AM GOING TO TURN THIS **PARK** INTO ONE BIG **FISH TANK**!
IT WILL BE A KINGDOM FIT FOR AN **OCTOPUS**!

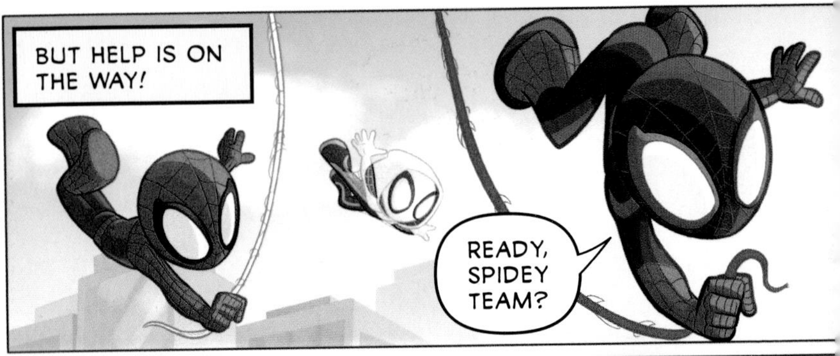
BUT HELP IS ON THE WAY!
READY, SPIDEY TEAM?

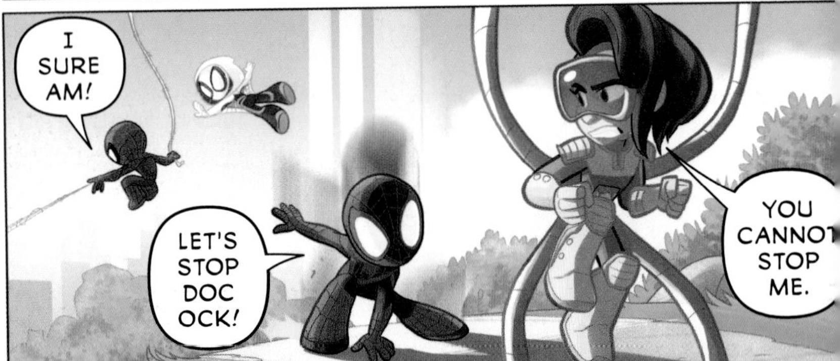
I SURE AM!
LET'S STOP DOC OCK!
YOU CANNOT STOP ME.

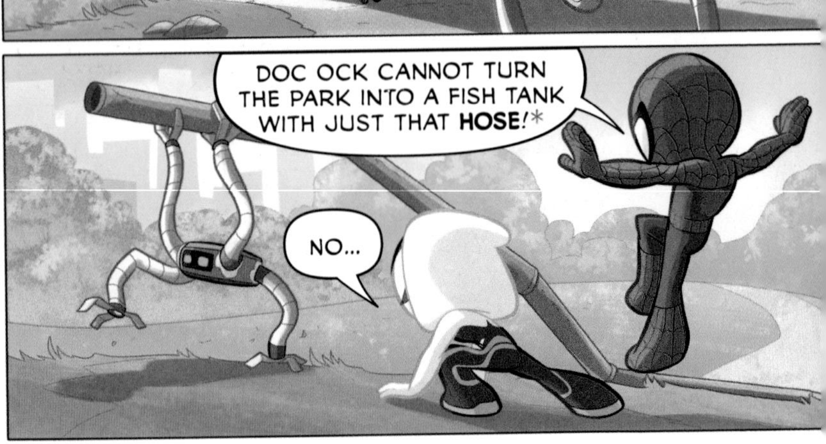
DOC OCK CANNOT TURN THE PARK INTO A FISH TANK WITH JUST THAT HOSE!*
NO...

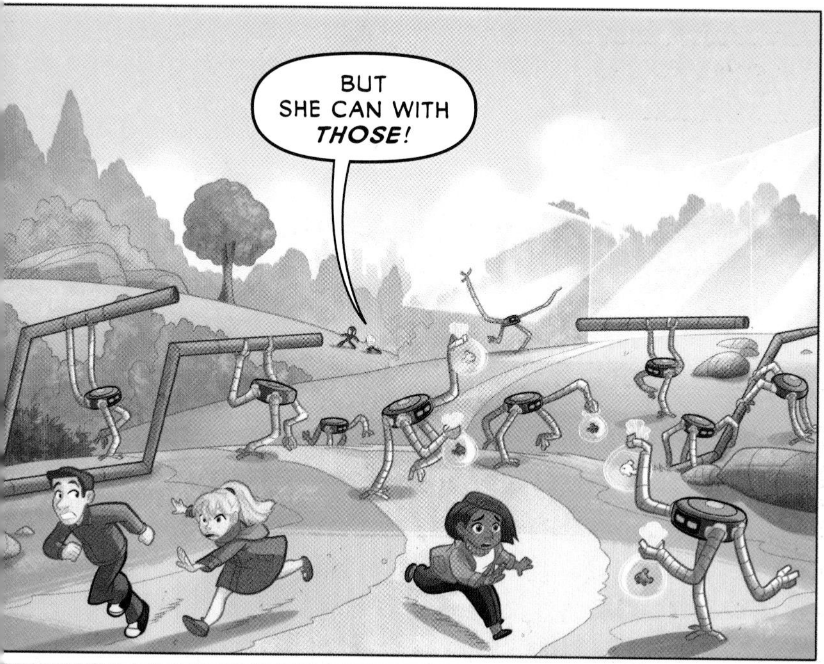
BUT SHE CAN WITH *THOSE!*

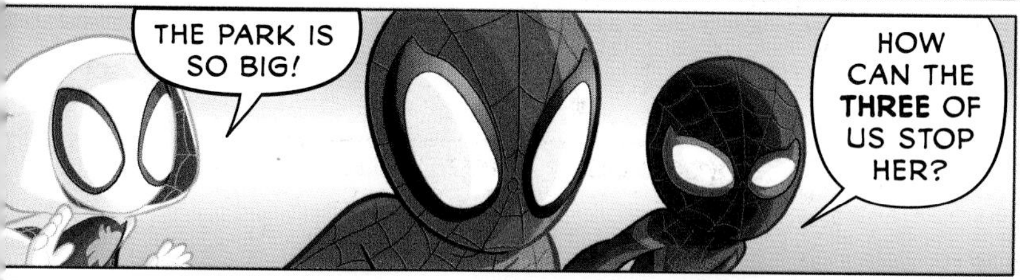
THE PARK IS SO BIG!
HOW CAN THE **THREE** OF US STOP HER?

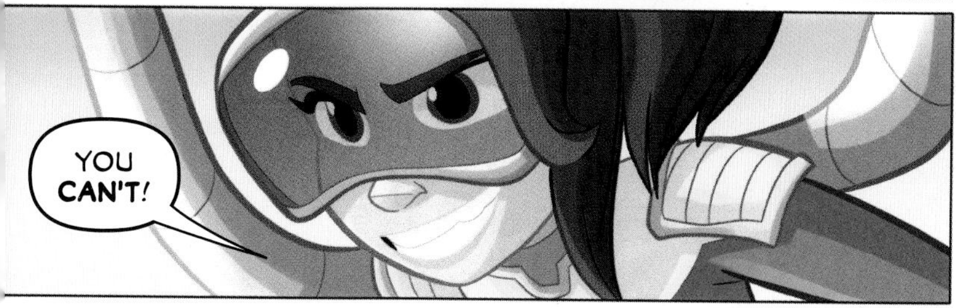
YOU **CAN'T!**

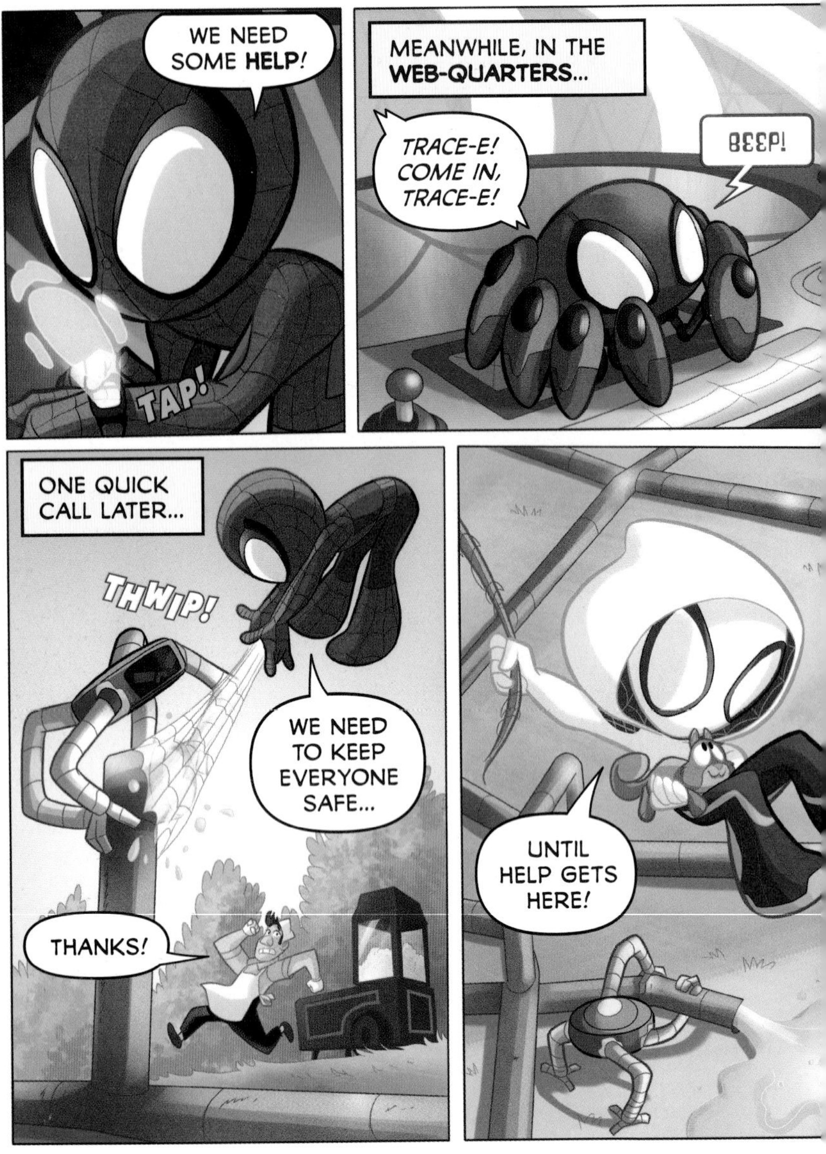
WE NEED SOME HELP!
TAP!
MEANWHILE, IN THE WEB-QUARTERS...
TRACE-E! COME IN, TRACE-E!
BEEP!
ONE QUICK CALL LATER...
THWIP!
WE NEED TO KEEP EVERYONE SAFE...
THANKS!
UNTIL HELP GETS HERE!

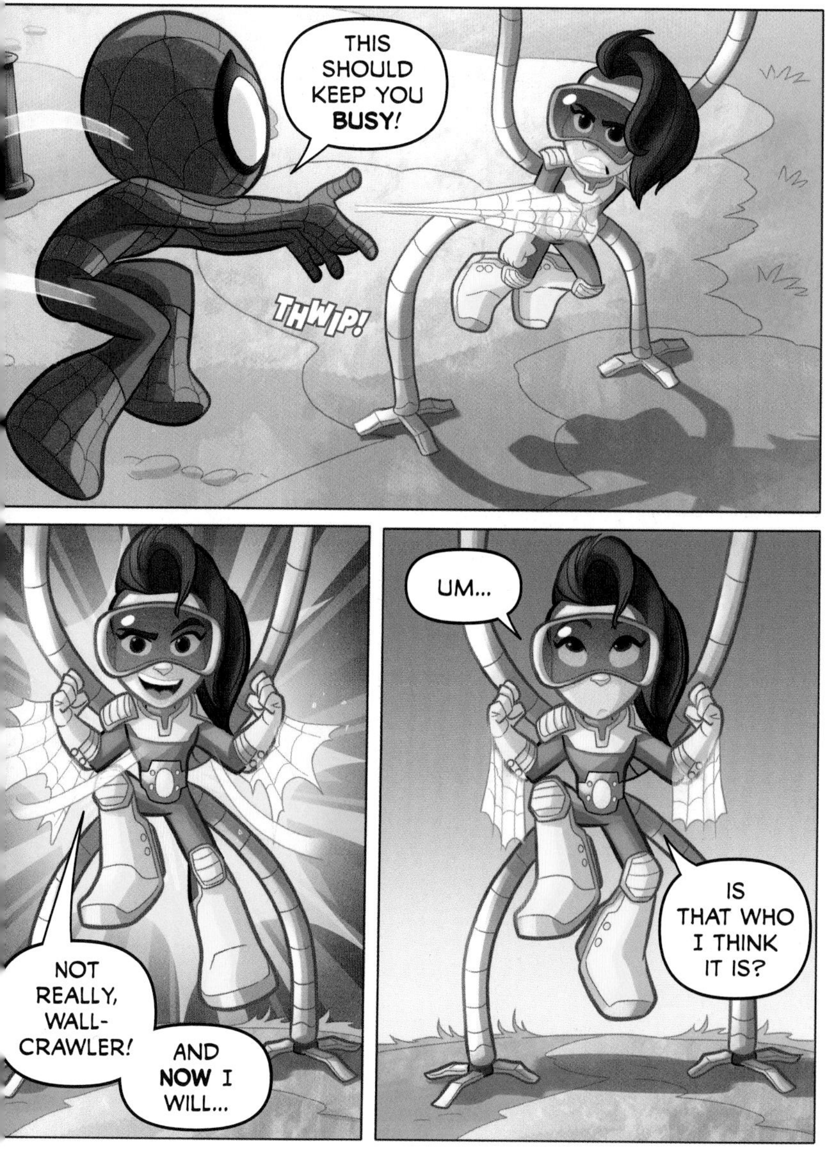
THIS SHOULD KEEP YOU BUSY!
THWIP!
NOT REALLY, WALL-CRAWLER!
AND NOW I WILL...
UM...
IS THAT WHO I THINK IT IS?

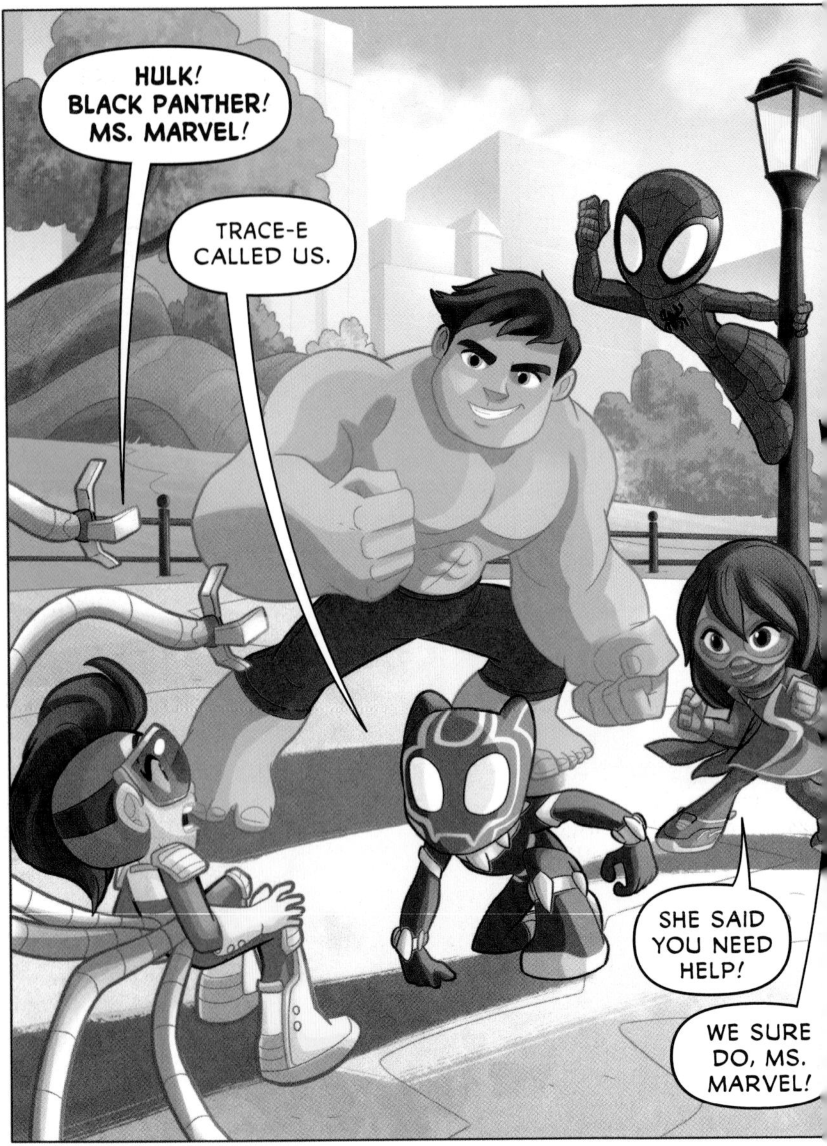
HULK! BLACK PANTHER! MS. MARVEL!
TRACE-E CALLED US.
SHE SAID YOU NEED HELP!
WE SURE DO, MS. MARVEL!

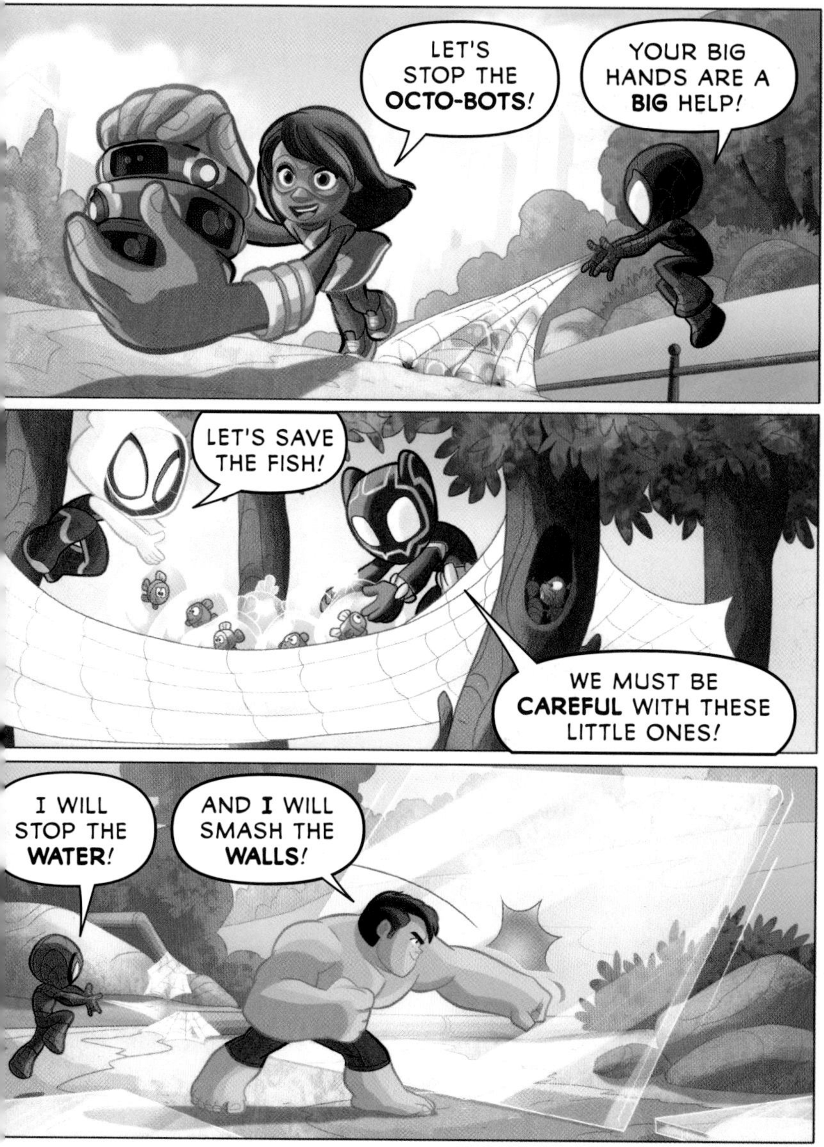
LET'S STOP THE **OCTO-BOTS**!
YOUR BIG HANDS ARE A **BIG** HELP!
LET'S SAVE THE FISH!
WE MUST BE **CAREFUL** WITH THESE LITTLE ONES!
I WILL STOP THE **WATER**!
AND **I** WILL SMASH THE **WALLS**!

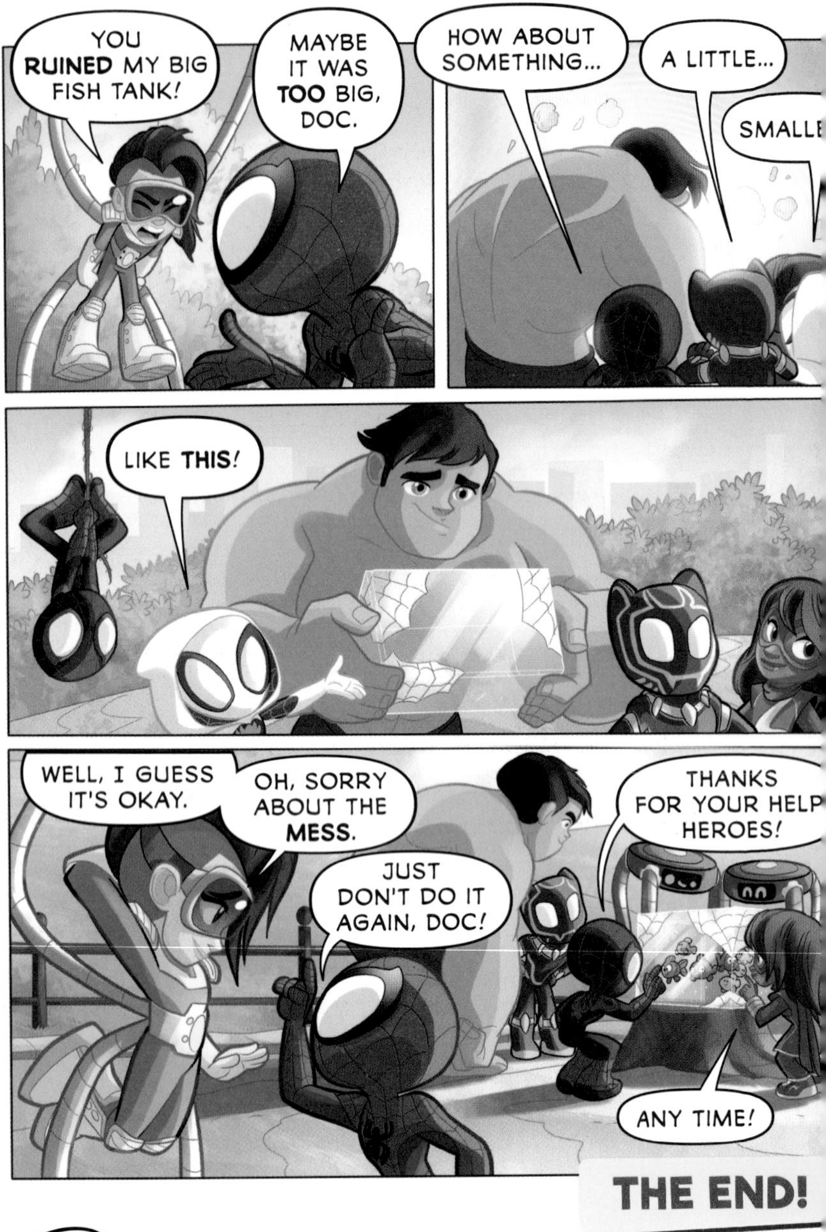
YOU RUINED MY BIG FISH TANK!
MAYBE IT WAS TOO BIG, DOC.
HOW ABOUT SOMETHING...
A LITTLE...
SMALLE
LIKE THIS!
WELL, I GUESS IT'S OKAY.
OH, SORRY ABOUT THE MESS.
JUST DON'T DO IT AGAIN, DOC!
THANKS FOR YOUR HELP HEROES!
ANY TIME!
THE END!

VOCABULARY WORDS

Some words in the *Spidey and His Amazing Friends* stories are marked with a ✱. Here is a list of those words and their meanings:

Spidey-alert – A warning that tells Team Spidey there is trouble

Web-quarters – Team Spidey's secret base

Cloaking power – Miles's ability to turn invisible

Spidey-sense – A feeling that warns Spidey, Ghost-Spider, and Miles of danger

Trap – A tool to catch and hold someone or something

Clues – Something that helps lead to solving a mystery

Thwip – The action of shooting a web

Pumpkin prank – An object used by Green Goblin to annoy Team Spidey

Invisible – Unable to be seen

Smash – To break something into lots of pieces

Library card – A piece of paper with your name on it that lets you borrow library books

Hose – A tube that allows water to pass through it

Script by **Steve Behling**
Layouts and cleans by **Giovanni Rigano**, **Antonello Dalena**
Inks by **Cristina Giorgilli**, **Cristina Stella**
Color by **Dario Calabria**, **Lucio De Giuseppe**
Cover and design by **Falcinelli & Co.**